# Gorgeous
### BOOK ONE

## **ALSO BY LISA SHELBY**

The You & Me Series
(a sweet and sexy series of adult contemporary standalones.)

You & Me

More

Something Just Like This

———

The Gorgeous Duet

Gorgeous: Book One

Gorgeous: Book Two

Visit
**WWW.LISASHELBY.COM**
to shop for these titles

also available at all major online retail outlets

# Gorgeous
### BOOK ONE

# LISA SHELBY

GORGEOUS
Copyright © 2018 Lisa Shelby Books, LLC
ISBN: 978-1983434020

This book is a work of fiction. Names, characters, businesses, places, events and incidents are either the products of the author's imagination or used in a fictitious manner. Any resemblance to actual persons, living or dead, or actual events is purely coincidental. All rights reserved. This book or parts thereof may not be reproduced in any form, stored in any retrieval system, or transmitted in any form by any means—electronic, mechanical, photocopy, recording, or otherwise—without prior written permission of the publisher, except as provided by United States of America copyright law. Except for the original material written by the author, all songs, song titles, and lyrics mentioned in Gorgeous: Book One are the property of the respective songwriters and copyright holders.

Cover Design, Interior Design & Formatting by:
Kiss & Tell Design Lab

Editing:
Finishing Touch Editing

Always for S.

Thanks for always sharing your moon with me, baby.

L

"Life isn't meant to be merely survived – it's meant to be *lived*."

~ Rachel Hollis

# TABLE OF CONTENTS

COPYRIGHT
DEDICATION
CHAPTER ONE .................................................................. 15
CHAPTER TWO ................................................................. 20
CHAPTER THREE ............................................................. 27
CHAPTER FOUR ................................................................ 33
CHAPTER FIVE ................................................................. 46
CHAPTER SIX .................................................................... 56
CHAPTER SEVEN .............................................................. 70
CHAPTER EIGHT ............................................................... 82
CHAPTER NINE ................................................................. 97
CHAPTER TEN ................................................................. 106
CHAPTER ELEVEN .......................................................... 118
CHAPTER TWELVE ......................................................... 129
CHAPTER THIRTEEN ..................................................... 140
CHAPTER FOURTEEN .................................................... 158
CHAPTER FIFTEEN ......................................................... 165
CHAPTER SIXTEEN ........................................................ 170
CHAPTER SEVENTEEN .................................................. 191
CHAPTER EIGHTEEN ..................................................... 205
CHAPTER NINETEEN ..................................................... 226
CHAPTER TWENTY ........................................................ 231
CHAPTER TWENTY-ONE ............................................... 249
PLAYLIST
ACKNOWLEDGMENTS
NEWSLETTER
ABOUT THE AUTHOR

## CHAPTER ONE

*Ronan*

Boredom.

I can't escape it.

It usually sets in earlier in the evening, but tonight's event is less painful than usual.

But, the boredom *has* set in.

It's no one's fault.

You've been to one charity gala...you've been to them all.

This one *is* better than most. It's elegant and classy yet somehow different than the norm. The band is actually pretty good, and the silent auction, surprisingly, has some unique and impressive items up for bid. My assistant can throw a mean gala, but whoever is in charge tonight, isn't too bad either. With Evelyn's impending retirement hanging over my head, maybe I should inquire to see just who *is* running the show here tonight.

As fine as the event may be, it's still the same old stuffed shirts and money men I see every time I attend one of these events.

This is my life.

The same meetings I attend at work each week. The same workout routine day in and day out. The same vapid women who only care about my name and my money. I seem to be stuck on the treadmill of life, and tonight doesn't appear to be changing my routine. This may be Portland and not San Francisco, but old men with money are the same no matter the city. At least Portland is a bit less stuffed shirt and a little more casual.

With the usual after-dinner monotony setting in and my donation made, it's time to find Dr. Evers, give him my best, and take my leave.

I join the good doctor and some of his colleagues, whom I met earlier in the evening, and clasp him on the shoulder. "Leo, you throw a great…"

My words are cut short by the sudden static in the atmosphere. When I move my line of sight ever so slightly to the left, I see the cause of the storm taking place in my chest at the same time my breath seems to falter. Across the room is a sight unlike anything I have ever seen.

Her chestnut hair is up, exposing the olive skin of her exquisite neck. She's too far away for me to see her eye color, but they're dark. Mysterious. Her smile...her smile is life-altering. She has the adorable elegance of Audrey Hepburn while being sexy and alluring at the same time.

Gorgeous.

Dr. Evers snaps me back to reality, although I'm not sure my reality will ever be the same. "Ronan, thank you for coming tonight. You were more than generous with your donation, and it's much appreciated. I hope you weren't coming over to say your goodbyes. The night is still young."

Seconds ago, saying good night had been my plan, but there is no way I'm leaving this ballroom without meeting her. I'm distracted and I know it's rude not to look Dr. Evers in the eye, but my actions are out of my control. I can't take my eyes off her.

"Not just yet. I think I need to take another trip around the silent auction and make sure I didn't miss anything. Thanks again for having me. You and your wife throw a great party."

Not waiting for his reply, I slowly make my way around the edge of the ballroom shadowing her as she works her way around the other side of the room. Watching her move is like watching a fine wine swirl around a glass. She is graceful and smooth, and damn, does she have legs. We both reach our opposite ends of the silent auction, and I watch her as she checks each table and makes notes on her tablet.

"Ronan, there you are!" Mrs. Evers sings as she approaches me. "What's tickling your fancy here, Mr. McKinley? You looking to bid on the trip to St. Barts?"

I didn't even realize there was a trip to St. Barts up for bid on the table in front of me. "Still deciding, Sheila. A man can't rush a decision this important. It's quite an impressive collection of items up for bid tonight. You've outdone yourself, as usual." I may be talking to Sheila, but every bit of my attention is focused solely on the woman now only one table over from where I stand.

"Ah, a very wise and decisive man. If I didn't know how focused you were with your work, I would wonder why you were still single. You really should make the time to meet someone and settle down."

"Maybe that wisdom and decisiveness is the exact reason I'm still single, Sheila." I don't continue because she's here. My mystery woman is now only a couple of feet away.

"Oh, Olivia, there you are! The night has been superb. Cheers to all of your hard work. I can't thank you enough, my dear."

*Olivia.*

"Mrs. Evers, I'm so glad to hear it, and it has been my pleasure! The auction has been a huge success. I was just checking all the tables, and we've raised more than I ever could have expected! Is there anything you or Dr. Evers need?"

Her voice...her voice sounds like the smoothest bourbon. Soothing. I could listen to her talk all night.

"Oh, we're just fine, but I would like you to meet someone who has been very impressed with your work here tonight." Standing stock-still, I'm not really hearing anything Sheila says, she has to take me by the arm and give me a little pull to place me in front of the most mesmerizing woman I have ever seen. "Olivia Adams, meet Ronan McKinley. Ronan was one of our biggest donors this evening."

I extend my hand, and when she places hers in mine, the rest of the world vanishes. I can see it in her eyes as well. There's some kind of chemical reaction happening here, and she upsets me in the best possible way. But I also see confusion in her gaze, and her smile fades.

Her eyes hold mine, and from this close, I can see a tiny scar above her eyebrow. Just as I had imagined, her eyes are brown. Dark, doe eyes that are mysterious and maybe even a little sad.

"It's a pleasure to meet you, Miss Adams." I give her a squeeze as my grip holds steady, not wanting the moment to pass.

Suddenly, the woman who had been so bubbly and personable to every person she crossed paths with a mere moment ago, seems quiet and shy.

"Very nice to meet you as well." She shakes her head, and her eyes quickly look down at the ground, and slowly she pulls her hand from mine. Clearly, she too is affected and can feel whatever this is between us.

With her eyes no longer where I can see them, I feel as though I'm being robbed of something precious. A gift. I need to see them again.

"Excuse me, Mrs. Evers, but I need to go help wrap up the auction. Please let me know if you need anything at all." For the briefest of moments her chocolate eyes find mine, but now there is something that seems fearful; as though she can't flee fast enough. "It was nice to meet you, Mr. McKinley. Have a lovely evening."

And just like that she's gone.

The feeling of want, need, and even possessiveness that takes over in the instant she walks away is irrational, yes, but there all the same.

## CHAPTER TWO

*Olivia*

My mind has been reeling since last night. I still can't take my mind off the events that have continued to replay in my head while getting from my car to the safety inside the elevator. My thoughts have my usual alert self off her game, and I startle when a man rounds the concrete column ahead of me, but much to my relief he takes the stairs.

I'm beyond grateful when the elevator doors finally open and even more so when the doors close, and I'm the only person inside. The parking garage underneath the hotel always makes me uncomfortable. I do my best not to live in fear, but I also try to always be aware of my surroundings. Once I start making my ascent to the fifth floor, where my office awaits, a smile finds its way to my face, and I can feel the excitement of last night all over again.

*"We did it, Alex! It went off without a hitch!"*

*Alex pulls me into a hug and squeals, "You did it, Olivia! It was all you. This was your baby, and it was perfect! Congratulations!"*

*I pull my shoes off and take a seat in the now empty ballroom, and it seems odd to think that such a short time ago this room was full of beautifully dressed people and amazing decor. Now, with the lights up and all of my hard work being torn down, the exhaustion sets in, and a case of delirium must follow because my mind keeps going back to* him. *I know his name, but thinking of him having a name makes it too real, and he is nothing short of a fantasy.*

*He seemed almost fictional. Like he had walked right out of some modern-day fairytale. It wasn't simply because he was tall with a broad build and dark features. Yes, he was incredibly handsome, but he also had a natural strength about him. You just knew upon meeting him that he was powerful. Everything about him was intense, and when he shook my hand and his eyes met mine, it felt like my entire world had shifted ever so slightly.*

*I know it was just an instant, but it was enough to have me running for the hills and escaping his presence as quickly as I could.*

"*I couldn't have done it without you, Alex. You taught me everything I know, and you were there every step of the way. Thank you for everything.*"

"*I wouldn't want to work with anyone else and you know it. Besides, I'm not the only person who was with you every step of the way. Don't think I didn't see mister tall, dark, and handsome following your every move last night. What was that all about and who was he?*"

"*What are you talking about, there was nobody following me around last night.*"

*I know it would be too good to be true, but how much would I love it to be Ronan McKinley she is talking about. Besides, she doesn't know what she's talking about.*

"*Don't tell me you didn't see him. I saw you shake his hand and after you walked away, he stalked you like his prey. Tell me you at least got his number."*

*"Alex, why would I get the number of a man who you are making up in your head? Ronan McKinley was not following me around the gala tonight. You must be crazy with exhaustion."*

*"Ha! I knew you knew who I was talking about!"*

*"Oh, stop it. You are living in a dream world."*

*"Huh. Well, you could have fooled me. He looked like he was pretty smitten. Fascinated at the very least. I mean, who could blame him? Look at you."*

*"I am nothing special, Alex. It's very sweet of you to try to boost my ego like you always do, though."*

*"Hey, I don't want to hear that again. Got it. You are incredibly special. Just because you look like Portland's version of Kate Beckinsale isn't the reason either. You are strong, independent, and you've been through things that most people wouldn't make it through and out on to the other side. You are special, and that fine-looking man knew it the moment he laid his eyes on you."*

The ding of the elevator reaching my floor clears my head of thoughts about last night and the possibility that a man like *him* could think anything complimentary about me. The smile is still on my face, and I love that, at the very least, I have the memory of the moment we met and the way he made me feel. It's not something that many women could easily dismiss. I am human after all.

Walking down the hall with a little extra spring in my step from a job well done and a handshake to beat all handshakes, I can't help but hum under my breath as I log into my computer and dial into my voicemail. Looking around my bare minimum space, with no personal items adorning it, I think to myself it might be nice to have a picture of *him* somewhere on my desk. But then again, I have a feeling just having a picture of *him* to stare at all day would be too distracting and not much work would get done.

I grab a pen and when the voicemail begins, I am too shocked to write a word of it down. In fact, I have to play it a second time to really take in what is being said.

"Hello, this message is for a Miss Olivia Adams. This is Evelyn Hunter calling from EVC Corp. Your gala last night has earned you rave reviews, and we are very interested in working with you. We would like to extend an invitation to interview for a position here at EVC. Please be on the lookout for a package to arrive in your name with hotel accommodations and a round-trip airline ticket to San Francisco. Please do not hesitate to call with questions."

The messaging system is asking me over and over again if I would like to delete or save my message, but I'm too shocked to push any of the buttons.

*What in the hell was that all about?*

Eventually, I hang up the phone and realize this must be some kind of joke, but I still search for EVC Corp online. At the top of the list is Exalt Venture Capital Corp, founded by Daniel and Patrick McKinley. A deeper dive into their homepage has my mouth hanging open as I stare at a picture of the President of Real Estate Development. Ronan McKinley's blue eyes have the same effect on me through my computer screen as they did in my dreams last night.

"Morning, superstar!" Alex chirps as she enters the office.

"Morning..."

"What's up with you? You look like you've seen a ghost."

"Not a ghost, but come here. Listen to this

voicemail."

Alex holds the phone to her ear, and I can see the confusion on her face. When I point to the picture on my screen, her eyes nearly bulge out of her head.

She hangs up and slowly her face lights up. "I told you so!"

"What are you talking about? You didn't tell me I was going to come in to a job offer from EVC Corp this morning."

"No, but I told you that man was smitten."

"Come on, Alex..."

"Hey, Olivia. Fed Ex for you."

Alex and I turn to each other and both start laughing hysterically because this just can't be what we think it is. John, from the mail room, looks at us like we've both just been released from the looney bin, drops the package on my desk, and leaves.

"No way, Alex. It can't be." I look at the delivery on my desk like I'll catch some rare disease if I touch it.

"Oh, but it has to be. Open it! Open it!" she begs, bouncing up and down in her heels.

"I can't. You do it!"

"You sure?"

I nod my assurance.

She picks up the delivery and tears back the tab. She pulls the envelope open and peeks in cautiously before pulling out several pieces of paper. "Olivia..."

Jumping out of my chair, I rip the papers from her hands. In my fingers, I now hold a plane ticket to San Francisco, a hotel confirmation to the St. Francis, and a written invitation to meet with the Senior Administrative Manager, Evelyn Hunter, about a position as a personal assistant/event planner to the President of the Real Estate Division of EVC Corp.

"Who does he think he is?" I say, pacing the office, waving the papers in the air. "How can he be so arrogant to think I would just give up my life here and move to San Francisco so I could work for him! Egotistical bastard!"

I throw myself into my chair and dial the number on the bottom of the letter. I nearly pound off the numbers on my phone I dial with such anger.

"EVC, this is Evelyn."

"Hello, this is Olivia Adams and..."

"So, nice to hear from you, Olivia. I hope this means you received your package?"

"I did..."

"Wonderful, I hope next Thursday works for you. We're looking forward to showing you a little bit about EVC and to see if we're a good fit for one another."

"I'm sorry, Evelyn, but I won't be able to make it next week. Thank you very much for the offer, but I'm quite happy where I am, and I'm not interested in a move right now. Again, thank you very much for your consideration, and I'll return the ticket today."

"That won't be necessary, Miss Adams. Please keep the ticket, but are you sure we can't convince you to change your mind? Mr. McKinley was very impressed with your work, and I think his offer would be quite impressive."

"Please give Mr. McKinley my sincere appreciation, but I'm really not interested. Have a nice day." I hang up the phone, shaking. All the while Alex stands next to me, looking dumbfounded.

*Did I really just do that?*

The rest of the day goes by in a blur.

By five o'clock, the day is over, but I don't recall a single conversation. Today has flashed by, and the only thing on my mind has been the man that has taken over my every thought.

I'm giving myself tonight, and then no more thinking about Ronan McKinley.

## CHAPTER THREE

*Olivia*

*Crap! Hot, hot, hot!*

The scalding hot coffee dripping down my arm is a testament to the day I'm having.

My car wouldn't start this morning, I was late to my first appointment, and the wedding that should be taking place this weekend has been called off because Scotty Clark couldn't keep it in his pants.

And now this...

I don't even know what I was thinking having coffee this late in the day to begin with. The last thing I need is another sleepless night.

The last two weeks I've been distracted. Off my game. I thought seeing Bryce this past weekend would knock some sense into me, but things were just like they always are.

Sweet.
Normal.
Boring.

Our relationship isn't bad, but there isn't much to it either. Bryce is obsessed with his work, and we only see each once a week, if that. It works for me, though. It's important to me to have my own life and to depend on only myself. Bryce feels more like a friend whom I occasionally have mediocre sex with. Come to think of it,

I felt more in the handshake I shared with *him* the night of the gala than I have ever felt in the three years I've been with Bryce.

Wiping the coffee from my blouse, I hear the phone on my desk ringing, and I nearly trip over the strap of my purse sticking out from underneath my desk as I lunge for my phone.

"This is Olivia," I huff on labored breath.

"Miss Adams, hello. This is Evelyn Hunter calling from EVC."

"Excuse me?"

*What is up with the universe today?*

"Miss Adams, we know that you weren't interested in coming to San Francisco to meet with us, but Mr. McKinley is in Portland next week and was hoping you might reconsider and meet with him for an interview to go over his open position."

"Really? Here in Portland?" I huff, still out of breath from my spill and near-death trip on my purse.

"Yes, Miss Adams. We can work around your schedule and make it after business hours if need be. Does six p.m. Monday evening work for you? I can send you the contract so you have time to look at the offer before you meet with Mr. McKinley."

"Things haven't really changed in the last two weeks, but I thank you once again for the offer, Ms. Hunter."

"Miss Adams, one meeting. That's all we're asking. Hear what EVC has to offer, and you're free to say no after. Mr. McKinley is very persistent when he has an idea about something. It may be in your best interest to accept the meeting invite and get it over with or he may never quit asking."

I don't know if it's the two weeks of sleepless

nights, the off-kilter day I'm having, or the threat of Ronan McKinley and his persistence, but I find myself uttering the last words I thought I would ever speak when I answered my phone.

"Sure, I'll meet with him. I want to make it clear in advance, though. I do not have any intention of accepting the position, but if the meeting will prevent the requests from continuing, then I'd be more than happy to meet with him."

"I'm happy to hear it, and I know he will be too. I'll get the contract over to you, and Mr. McKinley will see you at six o'clock Monday evening. I'll include the meeting address with the contract. Don't hesitate to call if you have any questions about the paperwork, Miss Adams. I'm more than happy to answer any questions you might have or put you in touch with our Human Resources team."

"Okay, did you need my email address?" I ask as a new email floats into my inbox.

"No, dear. I've got it, and I've already sent the contract your way."

"Yes, I see that. Thank you."

*And why do you have my email already? Creep much?*

"I was able to find your information on the hotel website. Made things very simple."

*That's right. She's sending to your work email not your personal email. Calm down, Olivia. This poor woman isn't stalking you.*

"Again, let me know if you have any questions, and Mr. McKinley will see you next week."

"Thank you."

The sound on the other end of the line goes dead. A few seconds later, I finally hang up the receiver and hold my head in my hands.

Can I hit the reset button and start this day over?

---

I called and verified the address with Evelyn, but I still feel like I'm in the wrong location as my heels tap along the dock of the Portland Marina in search of a boat called *The Jupiter*. I know I shouldn't be here, and I know I shouldn't have worn my favorite sheath dress and my highest heels. Yet, here I am.

I also know I'm not meeting *him* just so he'll stop offering me jobs. I know I'm here because I want to see him again. He isn't interested in me, and he isn't the kind of man I'm attracted to, but there is no denying he is a rare man indeed, and he looked at me like he could see right through me. He wants to hire me to work for him not date me. I need to remember that, no matter what Alex says.

When I told Alex about my call with Evelyn, she flipped out. She insists there was more to this than a job. She claims the way he watched me at the gala is all the proof she needs that he is definitely interested in me. She doesn't know what she's talking about, though. Olivia Adams and Ronan McKinley are not circling the same sun let alone spending time in the same solar system.

I pass a few more boats and notice they seem to be getting bigger. I stop short when I see the boat I'm looking for.

*The Jupiter*.

It's too much. What kind of job interview happens on a freaking boat? Correction, this isn't a boat; this is a luxury yacht. I can't do this. Just as I turn on my heels to flee the scene, I hear my name called from somewhere above me.

"Miss Adams, you made it!"

A smiling gray-haired man walks down the steps that lead to the yacht with his hand extended.

"Miss Adams, right this way. Mr. McKinley is expecting you." I shake his hand, and he wastes no time leading me onto the yacht. "The name's Lou, and I'm the captain of this pretty little lady. It's nice to have you aboard."

I follow behind him, and he leads me into the interior of the boat. The interior of the boat that is filled with dark wood, plush furnishings, and pieces of art that look to be worth enough that keeping them at sea wouldn't be the safest place for them.

"Can I get you a drink while you wait?" Lou asks, still smiling.

I like him.

"No, thank you. I'm fine."

"All right then, I'm gonna head back up to the wheelhouse, and Mr. McKinley should be with you soon."

Once alone with my thoughts, I feel my frustration start to grow and maybe even a little anger begin to bubble up inside me.

*Who does he think he is?*

This is not an appropriate place to conduct an interview, and if he thinks this setting, with all of his expensive things, is going to impress me, he is sorely mistaken. It's all kind of gross, really. All this boat does is steel my resolve to say no to his offer.

*What a jerk.*

"Miss Adams, thank you for accepting my invitation," he says from behind me.

Hearing his voice does something to me, but I'm still ready to get this interview over with. I swing myself around ready to hold my ground.

That ground I thought I would be standing firm on, falls out from under my feet the moment I see him standing in front of me in his perfect suit, with his perfect face, and his heart-stopping blue eyes.

My breath has been taken once again, and I have a feeling it's going to be a little harder to keep my steely resolve in place. I seem to have taken on more than I may have bargained for.

## CHAPTER FOUR

*Ronan*

I know watching her from the monitors back in the galley wasn't right, but I knew from my one experience in the presence of this woman that I needed to be ready for her impact before I came face to face with her.

Watching her disapproval at the setting of our meeting and seeing her scoff at some of the finery on board made me chuckle while spying on her. Although, this means the setting has had the opposite effect on her than I had hoped, it has also intensified my attraction for her. She isn't like the people I'm usually surrounded with, and it's refreshing.

Quietly entering the lounge, I catch her off guard with my greeting. "Miss Adams, thank you for accepting my invitation."

Witnessing her swing around full of piss and vinegar only to have her demeanor change and her breath hitch once she's facing me has an effect on me I am not sure I will ever forget. God, she is a thing of beauty, even though she is clearly pissed and feeling unsure of herself. I don't want her to feel uncomfortable, but I love that there is no denying she's feeling something too.

"Mr. McKinley..." she says sounding almost breathless.

I step closer to her and extend my hand. Just as before, the atmosphere changes, and sparks or connections or whatever the hell you want to call it take over. If only, just like before, she didn't lose that spunk of hers. The sparkle in her eyes fades a touch, and she once again closes herself off.

"Can I get you something to drink? I've been told dinner will be ready momentarily, but if I can get you something now, it's no bother at all."

"Dinner?"

Uh, oh. Evelyn told me she didn't think this plan would go over well after her brief conversations with Olivia, but as often is the case, I didn't listen. I need to find a way to dig myself out of this hole, so I use all the charm I can muster.

"Yes, it would have been rude to ask you to meet at this time of day and not provide you dinner. Common courtesy, wouldn't you say?"

"Mr. McKinley..."

I cut her off before she can protest. "Come, let's go to the upper deck and discuss the gala from a couple of weeks ago." I hold my hand out so she can walk in front of me, but she pauses and gives me a little side-eye that says, she doesn't quite trust me. I can't help but chuckle again as I pass her and let her follow behind me.

I know it's wrong, but her feisty, don't-mess-with-me attitude, is turning me on. I know the last thing she is trying to be right now is hot, but there isn't a damn thing she can do about that.

I stay quiet and do my best to clear my head now that she is no longer in view. I can feel her bristling behind me, and once we make it to the top of the stairs and the upper deck, I move to the side and usher her ahead of me.

I hear her gasp when she sees the candlelit setting waiting for us, and before she can speak, I jump into action.

"Miss Adams, your event for Doctor and Mrs. Evers was exceptional."

She stands a little taller and seems to be listening with a touch less bristle, but her chest is still heaving up and down with fiery passion at the vision of the candlelit table.

"As a businessman, who not only attends but also hosts many galas during the year, you could say I am an authority on the topic. And as an authority, let me say again, your gala was exceptional."

I pull her chair out for her, and I must have distracted her with my compliments because she takes the seat without protest. I don't want to waste the moment, so I fill her champagne glass without asking.

"Thank you for your kind words, Mr. McKinley, but I'm not sure I'm the right fit for you."

*Oh, I think you'd be just the right fit, Miss Adams.*

"I've never been a personal assistant, and I don't know that I really have a passion for the position."

*I'm sure I could find a position that fills you with passion, and oh how I would like the chance to try.*

"I understand your apprehension but, rest assured, you would still be planning events of many varieties and sizes. I have a very busy schedule and much of that entails attending and hosting everything from at-home dinner parties to art exhibits to the occasional fundraising gala. I have two administrative assistants to do most of the office work, but I need someone to keep my schedule running smoothly and provide event planning services."

Anna, the ships chief steward, arrives with the first course of our meal. She provides the details of our antipasto and leaves us on our own. Her presence seems to have brought the beautiful, candlelit dinner, flowers, and champagne back to mind.

Sitting back in her chair, arms crossed in front of her and her mouth tight, she speaks her mind. "This does not seem like the appropriate setting for a job interview, Mr. McKinley."

Independent. Strong. Proud.

She's pissed and for all the right reasons. She's a wild one, and I couldn't be more impressed.

"Well, it has been five days now with no answer. I know Evelyn sent you the contract and details about the job and since you had not accepted as of yet, I figured it was time to pull out the big guns."

Leaning forward, her hands land on the table, and she looks almost disgusted. "This feels more like a date than a job interview."

"I didn't mean to offend you, Miss Adams."

She sits back with her arms relaxed on the chair. "I'm not offended, Mr. McKinley, but I want to be clear, crystal clear...I only have intentions of keeping the evening professional."

"Of course, Miss Adams."

Feeling more at ease after stating her case, she takes her first bite of the food in front of us and seems non-plussed, and all I can do is watch her beautiful mouth as she eats. All of me wants so much more than to keep tonight professional.

"You've seen the contract details, but let's discuss the nuts and bolts of it, shall we? If there is anything you have questions or concerns about, please do not hesitate to stop me."

She nods and takes a drink of her champagne.

"In the past, my admins have shared duties. After

much discussion with Evelyn, we've come to the realization that she really has been acting more like my personal assistant while Allison and Leslie do most of the day-to-day admin work. With Evelyn's impending retirement, we've decided to call the position what it is, a personal assistant. Keeping in mind many of the duties will be planning my events both local and out of town."

She's sitting back in her chair with her glass in her hand, and even though I know she isn't meaning to, she looks seductive as hell.

*Keep it professional, McKinley.*

"I know the contract went over your pay and clothing allowance. Do you have any questions about those figures?"

"No, sir."

She's not giving me much to go on, so I push forward.

"I head the real estate division of EVC, and our focus is on building with sustainable products. Although, many of the events will be EVC related, I also have a love of art and attend many gallery openings and events connected to the art world. I would ask that you travel for business regularly."

"Would I be required to travel for dinners or just events that I am planning?"

"No, just the events you are planning from top to bottom."

"Why me?" she asks suspiciously.

*Because I have an unhealthy need to be near you.*

Telling her the truth, even if it is only a partial truth, I answer her simple question. "I was beyond impressed with the Evers gala and heard only positive reviews about the evening. With Evelyn's departure on the horizon, I will need the best to replace the best."

She sits up straighter in her seat.

"And to be honest...there is something about you, Miss Adams. I think the two of us would work well together."

"Mr. McKinley, we don't come from the same worlds. I can plan an event, but I'm not sure I'll have the connections you need."

"Evelyn can help you and so can I."

"Sir, not to be rude, but this all seems too good to be true."

"Well, you will have to spend a lot of time with me. There is always that down side."

This earns me a hard-fought smile, and it was more than worth the fight.

Our main course is delivered, the conversation slows, and after her first couple of bites, she puts down her knife and fork and sits back and sighs heavily.

"I really like where I'm at, and I'm not sure I want to move to San Francisco. Money isn't important to me. All of this..."—she motions with her arms to the vessel we're sitting on—"doesn't really appeal to me. Think of all the people you could help with the money it costs just to staff and maintain this yacht. I guess to me that old tried and true saying, *less is more,* is more my speed."

"Well, Miss Adams, I am fortunate enough to have the money to spend on a boat like this *and* also to do lots of charitable work. Most of my events are to raise money for projects that mean something to me."

Yes, I am defending myself, but that is only because I find her incredibly refreshing. It is rare to meet someone with values in my world. I don't know why, but I need her to come work for me. Yes, she's beautiful, but I've spent my life around beautiful women, and this woman outshines the rest. There is more to her than her beauty; she is almost ethereal. Something about her is causing me to need her like I have never needed anything or anyone before.

Of course, only in the most professional way.

---

*Olivia*

It's as if he knows I need the money, and I have an insurmountable amount of student loans to pay off. I mean it's all simply too good to even dream true. Besides, there is too much attraction, on my side at least, and it wouldn't be a safe move. Dream job or no dream job, it's not safe to work for a man I feel such an attraction to.

I am drawn to him, yet he is everything I don't find attractive in a person, let alone a man. This fact should make it easy to do the job and not fall head over heels for him at the same time.

*I can do this.*
*Right?*

Am I going to take this job? Have I just decided, sitting at a candlelit table on a yacht with Mr. Egotistical, that I'm taking this job and moving to San Francisco? There may be a cool breeze coming off the river, but I can feel a nervous sweat begin to coat my body.

There is no way I'm letting him know tonight. I can't let him think that the wining and dining is the reason I take the job. I refuse to inflate his ego any more than it clearly already is.

"Mr. McKinley..." I say, sliding my chair back with a screech and standing abruptly. "Thank you for the meal, but I'm going to need to think about this."

"We haven't had dessert yet."

"No dessert for me, thank you. I'll let you know in the morning what I decide."

"Please do and when you say yes, I'll need you to start Monday."

"Excuse me?"

He stands from the table, reaching into the inside pocket of his suit jacket. His suit jacket that is tailored perfectly, as is his white button-down shirt, sans tie and open at the top where his neck has been exposed all night.

Teasing me.

Taunting me.

"There is no need to wait, Miss Adams. I have an event in New York next week, and even though it's already planned, you can come and Evelyn will show you the ropes."

"What's the event?"

"I'll let you know when you call to accept."

*Oh, the arrogance of this man.*

"I'm sorry, sir, but I cannot *not* give two weeks. I owe my current employer at least that much."

"Do you have any events on your schedule that you're taking the lead on or that you wouldn't be able to hand over to someone else?"

*Infuriating! This man is infuriating!*

"Well, since I haven't made up my mind yet, what I have on my schedule isn't really your concern, now is it, Mr. McKinley?"

He smiles.

*What an arrogant jerk.*

He hands me the business card he pulled out of his jacket. "Call me when you decide. Here's my card." When his fingers touch mine, I feel it again. That energy that surges through my entire body and scares the hell out of me.

*I have to get out here!*

I grab my purse off my chair and rush toward the stairs down to the main deck of the boat. Before making my way down the stairs, I turn back to the stunning man who, by the look on his face, knows his touch affected me. The man who already assumes I'm going to take his job offer.

*Did I say he was infuriating?*

I cannot get off this God-forsaken boat fast enough. He is pretentious and disarming. I don't know why I let him get to me, but he does something to me that scares me to death.

Walking through the marina, I can't help but feel I'm being watched, and I refuse to turn around. I'm not sure what it would mean if I did find him watching me walk away or what effect it would have on my decision, but I will not allow myself to look back.

When I finally reach my car, I plop down into the driver's seat, slam the door just a little too hard, and rest my head on my steering wheel. I need a moment to think about what just transpired. Did he really think he needed to impress me with a candlelit dinner on a yacht? I mean, he is already offering to pay me three times what I'm currently making, and I don't do too badly for myself as it is. Throw in a clothing allowance, travel, and the array of events I would get to plan, and this job is a dream come true.

But do I want to move to San Francisco? I would say, what about Bryce, but when I mentioned the offer to him the other day, he didn't seem fazed by it one little bit. He said he was proud of me and that I should do what makes me happy. He said the distance wouldn't change anything, and I can't help but think how right he is.

What is there to change? We talk on the phone, see each other maybe once a week, and that's it. I don't feel emotionally connected to him as a boyfriend, but I would certainly miss his friendship. It's a little sad to think I've been in a relationship for three years, and a move to San Francisco isn't something that will rock the boat. We should be in a different place. *I* should be in a different place. I'm twenty-nine years old. If there was ever a time for a change this is it. Besides, Oregon still has me looking over my shoulder a little too much. California might be a nice fresh start.

Looks like I'm moving to San Francisco.

---

"Good morning, Miss Adams."

*He has my number programmed into his phone already? Creeper.*

"Good morning, Mr. McKinley."

"Have you come to a decision then?"

"I have, sir. I've decided to take you up on your offer, but I will not be able to join you in New York. I owe my current employer better than a few days' notice, and I do not want to leave them on bad terms. If this is a deal breaker, I understand and appreciate the offer."

Silence fills the other side of the line for many long seconds. It appears he really is used to getting what he wants.

*Well, the thought of paying off those student loans was nice while it lasted.*

"It's not ideal, Miss Adams, but if those are your terms, we can work around them. I find it quite admirable that you would risk this new opportunity due to your loyalty to your current employer, and it assures me I'm making the right decision by hiring you. I hope we at

EVC will also elicit the same loyalty from you."

"Of course."

"As you know, your relocation is covered, but should you need any assistance with your move or any information about the city, don't hesitate to ask. You have my number and, of course, Evelyn is available to assist. We'll be putting you up at the St. Francis until you find something so, no rush at all."

"That's very kind of you, sir."

"It's not kind, Miss Adams. We're asking you to move six hundred and fifty miles from home. The least we can do is make sure you're comfortable. I also don't want you to settle. Be sure to take your time researching different areas of town and find a location you're comfortable with. The last thing we want is for you to regret your decision."

I have never experienced a phone call that has confused me more than this one. It is nothing but professional, which is an incredible relief, but the kindness and concern he's showing me makes me feel much more than relief. I know it shouldn't, but it feels good. To have a man, not just any man, but Ronan McKinley, show concern for your general well-being, is something that feels incredible. My head knows he is speaking as a businessman who takes care of his employees, but the butterflies in my stomach are making more of the situation and throwing themselves into quite the little tizzy.

And I don't even like him!

"Thank you, Mr. McKinley. I'm sure I'll be fine, but I do appreciate your offer. I'll reach out to Evelyn if I have any questions or concerns."

"You're welcome. I look forward to working with you, and I'll see you a week from this coming Monday.

Have a nice day, Olivia."

The phone disconnects, and after a few seconds of repeating the sound of his luxurious voice saying my first name over and over in my head, I set my phone down.

*Get it together! He is your new boss, and all he did was say your name!*

Am I making a mistake?

The pay and the benefits are amazing. The chance to travel and expand my résumé is a once-in-a-lifetime opportunity. A move may be just the change I didn't even know I needed, but is it a mistake?

They way my body reacts when simply hearing his voice over the phone is a complete rush. Ronan McKinley is everything I can't stand in a person, and I don't know him from Adam, so why am I reacting this way?

Maybe it's the attention?

As much as I may enjoy my relationship with Bryce, he doesn't pay me a lot of attention. At first, I thought it was just what I needed. A man who had his own life and didn't expect me to change everything about my life to conform to his. I still get my much-needed alone time, but I see him often enough to feel like I am a part of a couple, and I know he would be there for me if I needed him.

That's always been enough for me, but I have to be honest with myself and admit his lack of caring about me moving to San Francisco, doesn't feel great. Yes, he said he would miss me, but he certainly didn't fight for me to stay. He was happy for me, told me what a great opportunity it was for me, and would support any decision I made.

I know Bryce well enough to know he wasn't trying to be hurtful, but it did hurt. I may be an independent woman who likes her space, but it doesn't mean there isn't a small part of me that wants to be fought for. To be missed enough that the person who claims to love you is a little sad you're leaving. Bryce didn't give me any of this, but I also don't feel any of these things about leaving Bryce either.

Maybe the move will be good for our relationship. We may appreciate each other more and miss our time together.

Only time will tell.

## CHAPTER FIVE

*Olivia*

"EVC, Ronan McKinley's office. This is Olivia speaking," I answer the call ringing on line one, and the nerves I feel from the simple task are irrational but there none-the-less. The call is patched through to Mr. McKinley's office and done quickly enough.

I don't think he's in just yet, but I do remember Evelyn saying his calls would ring to his cell if he wasn't in the office. I've been here for two hours already, and she's given me a plethora of information, but I am pretty sure I am remembering this detail correctly. To get the lay of the land, we're starting here at the front desk, and then I'll move back to my office, right next to *his*. I think I'll like it better out here.

"That was perfect. I know you're nervous but no need to be. You're doing great," Evelyn reassures me. I knew I liked her on the phone, but meeting her in person has caused my undying love to blossom.

She is a one-woman, well-oiled machine. She can do this job with her eyes closed while not seeming bored in the least. The part that has caused the blossoming love is the maternal instinct that she can't help but exude. She is kind, warm, motherly, and everything I ever dreamed of in a mother. I can't help but feel an instant connection to her.

I'm not sure what is happening to me. Gone is the woman who has expertly spent her life avoiding closeness with others. I don't have many emotionally connected relationships in my life, but Evelyn Hunter—and much to my dismay my new boss—have made me feel more than I'm used to in a very short span of time.

Even if the feelings are irritation, anger, and annoyance, *he* has still managed to bring out many different emotions from this disconnected woman. One of the strongest is the pull of attraction I feel for the egotistical jerk. Thank goodness, he isn't here yet. I haven't had to come face to face with him this morning. God forbid, he come into the office before noon.

Typical.

He is probably president of the real estate division by name only. It is a family-run business after all. He probably rolls into the office whenever he gets around to it, if at all. Living off the family wealth and living on luxurious yachts.

Yuck.

Evelyn is a great teacher, and her finely crafted organization and processes make everything easy to grasp. She even explained all of my HR documents, including my Non-Disclosure Agreement, in a way that made sense and seemed a little less daunting.

I'm concentrated on the spreadsheet on my computer screen, studying the details of Evelyn's vendor contacts, when I hear a disgusted grunt aimed in my direction.

"Who the hell is this?"

The gruff voice startling me from my work belongs to an older gentleman. He is short, stout, red-faced, and clearly not happy to see me here.

"Mr. McKinley, this is Olivia Adams. She'll be

filling my role once I've retired. Today is her first day. Olivia, please meet the CEO of EVC, Daniel McKinley."

I reach out my hand and am met with a grunt as he dismisses me and stalks down the hall, leaving me feeling foolish and quickly dropping my hand.

"Excuse my brother. He didn't get the manners in our gene pool. Welcome to the family. My name is Patrick. I'm that yahoo's baby brother and CFO of EVC."

Patrick McKinley, the taller and more attractive brother, offers his hand and offers me a warm smile that seems genuine. It's clear he's spent much of his life apologizing for his big brother.

"Nice to meet you, Mr. McKinley."

"Please, dear, call me Patrick. No need for formalities. We're all on the same team here."

"Thank you, sir. I'm excited to contribute to the team, and I hope I can be even half as competent as Evelyn. She's leaving me some pretty big shoes to fill."

"Oh, you're doing great, Olivia. You're going to breathe a breath of fresh air into this place," Evelyn says with a pat to my shoulder.

"I'm sure you'll do a great job. Evelyn doesn't give her approval to just anyone. Besides, your new boss was fortunate enough to get the family genes containing manners and common decency. At least you met my brother on a good day." He winks, letting me in on his joke. "Nice to meet you and welcome to EVC. I better go make sure he hasn't brought his son to taking the drink already. It's only eleven a.m. after all. We don't want him pissed before noon." He starts down the hall but yells over his shoulder. "But who would blame him when he's been left alone with Daniel for at least two minutes. That'd drive anyone to drink!"

He chuckles to himself before he joins his brother

and apparently his nephew, in the lion's den.

"Well, you've met the McKinley brothers." Evelyn smiles warmly.

"I sure have," I concur, wanting to ask why I didn't know that *he* was here. That bit of information gave me more of a scare than his cranky father did by a mile. I feel overtaken by dread, and I'm suddenly fidgety and anxious.

"You'll get used to Daniel, and luckily Patrick is usually there to balance him out. Never take his mood personally and you'll be fine. Patrick was right, though. Ronan takes after his uncle and not his father. I couldn't have been happier working for him, and if I didn't dream of traveling and spending time with my grandchildren, I may just stay forever. Now, where were we?"

Thirty minutes later, the elder brother passes by us wordlessly and walks out the tall glass doors that lead to the bank of elevators in the lobby. I think I prefer him walking by silently rather than him feeling the need to stop and talk. I have a feeling silence is golden when it comes to the elder McKinley brother.

Another ten minutes pass before the friendlier of the two is walking past the front desk.

"Olivia, hang in there and take good care of that nephew of mine."

Why does his request have a completely different connotation in my head than what am I sure he means?

"I'll do my best, sir."

Ugh...my mind is rapidly thinking of the many different ways I could take care of *him*.

*Stop it, you perv! You don't even like the arrogant jerk!*

He continues to the glass doors, and as he pushes the doors open, he pauses to shout in our direction.

"Evelyn, don't you go and retire on us without a proper goodbye. You two ladies have a grand day."

As he walks out, a cute red-haired delivery guy from Tommy's Joynt, if his shirt doesn't lie, is here with a large bag of food.

"Hey, you're new here." The ginger wags his eyebrows and looks me up and down. "The name's Aaron, and yours?"

Grabbing the clipboard from him, she doesn't even have to look at the paper she's signing and hands it back to him a second later. "Aaron, put your tongue back in your mouth and leave poor Olivia alone. Olivia, this is Aaron, and he works down at Tommy's Joynt, Ronan's favorite deli. He can be a handful, so we just have to do our best to keep him in line, don't we Aaron."

"Evelyn, this lovely little lass can keep me in line anytime she likes."

"Great first impression, boy. Give me the bag and be on your way." She holds her hand out, and when he doesn't move, she snaps her fingers to get his attention off me, but it doesn't work. He continues to stare as he hands her the bag.

He walks backward toward the doors, and with his hand over his heart, he laments, "Until we meet again, my dear Olivia."

Evelyn shakes her head, and I can't help but to giggle. I have a feeling Aaron is a handful like Evelyn says, but also all talk and no real bite.

"You are certainly getting to know the entire cast of characters today, lucky you," Evelyn says with a smile on her face and in her voice.

"He's harmless enough, I'm sure." I smile back.

"Yes, harmless but sure to put a smile on your face. Now, let's go see how Ronan's day is going and bring him lunch."

"I didn't even realize he was here until his dad and uncle got here," I say, hoping to hide the nerves that are now rushing back at the thought of seeing him again.

"Ronan was in by six a.m. this morning. He's always busy, but more than the norm at present. He has some big deals wrapping up this week, and he doesn't peek his head out too often at times like this. He works hard, that one. In fact, there are many nights he stays here all night and never goes home. He certainly doesn't rest on the family name; he's earned everything he's got."

And cue the guilt train. Everything I was thinking in my head about him a short hour ago has been shot down, and it appears *he* is the exact opposite of what I assumed.

*What is it they say about people who assume? Yep, I'm an ass.*

Evelyn knocks on the big wooden door, waits a beat, and pushes the door open.

The office is large and surprisingly homey. There is multihued carpet with dark furnishings that include a sitting area with a dark brown leather sofa, two large leather chairs, and coordinating coffee table and end tables. There is a small meeting table for four off to the side, and to the right is a large mahogany desk. The desk may be impressive, but it pales in comparison to the man behind it. The light from the floor to ceiling windows does nothing but add a glow to his lightly tanned skin and silky black hair.

*I wonder if that's a natural tan or if there are tan lines? Maybe he's a golfer? Wait, this is San Francisco. The clouds probably prevent a sun-kissed tan. Yep, it's natural.*

*Oh, my God. I am losing my mind!*

He looks up and smiles when he sees us entering the room.

"Will the conference table work for lunch today?"

"That would be great, Evelyn. You don't have to set it up, though. I've got it."

"Sounds good. I'll leave you to it."

I start to follow Evelyn out of the room when his deep voice stops me. "Miss Adams, please join me for lunch."

*I am clearly losing my mind!*

I know I didn't hear him correctly, so I embarrassingly have to ask him to repeat himself. "I'm sorry, sir. What was that?"

"Join me for lunch. It's your first day, and I want to see how you're getting along. I asked Evelyn to order plenty and legally, you do get a lunch break. So, if you wouldn't mind joining me?"

"Olivia, you know where to find me," Evelyn says, leaving the room and closing the door behind her. Effectively, leaving me on my own with *him* and staring blindly at the door as if she's going to pop back in and yell, gotcha! Oh, how I wish this was all just a prank.

"I wasn't sure what you would like, so I had Tommy's send me one of each of their boxed lunches as well as their broccoli salad, mac salad, and some mixed vegetables. Whatever we don't eat we'll put in the break room. So, what will it be?"

He's emptying out the bag and setting the food up on the table and speaking as casually as can be. He looks up and seems to recognize my hesitation.

He clears his throat. "I seem to have taken you off guard, Miss Adams. I should have asked if you had other plans for your first day." He's back to his slightly more formal self.

"No, no. I'm fine. Just surprised is all. Thank you very much for thinking of me," I manage to get out. I join him at the table and look at the different boxes and select the turkey sandwich box lunch.

"Please, take a seat. I'll get the rest of this out of the way and join you." He pushes the many options to the side of the table as I open my lunch box that is complete with a half a sandwich, pickle, chocolate chip cookie, and a bag of chips. A simple deli lunch like anyone would eat. Nothing posh. Nothing extravagant. I really did assume incorrectly.

"So, how's the first day going?"

"Fine, sir. Thank you for asking."

"Please, call me Ronan. Is it all right if I call you Olivia or do you prefer Miss Adams?"

"Olivia is fine, Mr. McKinley."

"Well, Olivia. We will be working together a lot, so I do hope that at some point you grow comfortable enough to call me by my first name, but whatever makes you comfortable works for me."

"Thank you, sir."

"I hope you're finding the accommodations at the Saint Francis to your liking?"

"It's absolutely beautiful. I could stand in the lobby and stare at those beautiful ceilings all day. Thank you for putting me up at the hotel, and I assure you I will be into my own place just as soon as possible."

"Take your time. We have a corporate discount there. It's no problem at all." He winks and the bite I have just taken nearly falls from my mouth.

"Thank you, sir." I can feel the blush creep up my neck when I call him sir again. I don't know why I can't call him by his first time, but it just feels too casual and a casual relationship with a man like *him* is the last thing I need.

As if reading my mind, he changes the subject to the dinner party this coming weekend at his home and things become much more professional, and my discomfort melts away. I'm surprised to find him very involved in the planning of the dinner and to see how much he cares about how well it goes.

"Since this is a dinner to celebrate the hard work of my senior management team, I want to be sure to pull out all the stops. I don't usually entertain at home, but my team is like family, and so I thought it would be the best setting to show them my appreciation."

I must admit, I can't wait to see his home. I know it sounds silly, but I can't help but to be curious about where a man like *him* calls home.

Before I know it, lunch is over and we've actually had a productive meal with me getting a feel for what he's expecting for his dinner party as well as some of his expectations of my job. We work well together, and I like all of his ideas. He's very hands-on, but we seem to have some kind of synergy already, and it's helping to ease my concerns.

There is still an attraction there, but there is also a professionalism and care about the work, on both sides. I think I may have made a good decision after all.

"Well, I better get back to work, and don't forget, you have a conference call in fifteen minutes, Mr. McKinley," I say, starting to clean up the table and pretending I didn't see the ghost of a smile play at his lips when I called him Mr. McKinley again. "I'll take the extra lunches to the break room and get out of your way."

He grabs the bag of extra food before I can. "Nah, that's okay. I've been stuck in this office since six o'clock this morning. It will do me some good to take the walk."

Yep, my assumptions about him were way off base. I feel a little sheepish even if I hadn't shared my thoughts aloud.

As we're walking out of his grand office, I notice a closed door in the back corner, and I must show my curiosity more than I intend to, because he feels the need to explain.

"Home away from home, I guess you could say. I work a lot and sometimes I have meetings at various times due to the different time zones our projects are happening in. There's a bed and bath back there for the occasions I need to sleep here, and fortunately there is the company gym downstairs. Sometimes I work from my home office if I know I have an early meeting. It just depends on my schedule."

"Oh, I...I...see," I say, stuttering on my words.

There just may be more to this man after all.

Just my luck.

## CHAPTER SIX

*Olivia*

Feeling anxious and a little too excited to see where a man like *him* lives, I fidget in the backseat all the way to my destination. When my town car pulls up to a beautiful brick home in Pacific Heights, I instantly fall head over heels in love.

Stepping out of the car, I take my time admiring the elegant brick building with its large glass doors decorated with ornate, black, wrought iron. I've never seen wrought iron look so beautiful and not in the least bit intimidating. The house is large and clearly luxurious yet somehow manages to have a quaint look to it that would indicate a lovely little family lives inside.

Finally forcing myself to take the steps toward the beautiful front door, I'm met by Evelyn before I have a chance to ring my arrival.

"There you are, my dear. I saw you on the monitors, and I worried you were thinking you were at the wrong address when I saw how slowly you were moving." She gives me a wink that says she knows I was admiring the beautiful home and am in a state of awe. "You're in the right place. Welcome. You'll get to know Franklin Street, as we refer to it, rather well as Ronan does work and entertain here from time to time."

I follow her through the entry and into a foyer of

dark wood floors and cream rugs. The walls are cream on the top and have a wainscoting of dark wood that matches the doors and crown molding at the ceiling. There is an ornate staircase of the same dark wood to the right that leads upward. I know this *is* a person's home and not an exhibit, but I so badly want to go exploring.

I trail on Evelyn's heels as she shows me the rest of the downstairs which includes a masculine, yet graceful and chic, dining room and sitting room, and a kitchen to die for.

The kitchen is more than just a nice kitchen; it is a room and has a feel all unto itself. The same dark floors carry through to the kitchen, but the rest of the room is all white and gray. Although the house is well over one hundred years old, and the kitchen shows it, it is still the most beautiful kitchen I have ever seen. Whites and grays against the dark floors give it a light, elegant, country feel. And the best part of the room is that it leads to a large outdoor deck that dreams are made of.

If most of my time will be spent on the main floor where the entertaining takes place, this is just fine by me. I don't know who could need more than this.

"Ladies, so nice to see you both on this fine day," *he* says entering the room. The massive kitchen feels as though it's shrinking with his presence. Even though the room was already filled with cooks and servers preparing for this evening's dinner, it still felt vast until *he* entered. "Olivia, I hope you found us without any problems?"

As my first week at EVC carried on at lightning speed, *he* eventually started calling me Olivia and has continued to ask me to call him by his first name as well, but I haven't gotten there yet. He is generally a formal person, but I do notice he is less formal with Evelyn and those he works with directly.

"No trouble at all, sir. You have a beautiful home."

"Thank you. Now, what can I do to help?" he asks, rubbing his hands together as if he can't wait to get started.

"Don't be silly. We've got everything under control. Now, leave us to it," Evelyn says, shooing him away with her hands.

"Okay...okay. I'll leave you alone, but please do let me know if you need anything. I can lift heavy things, and I can reach things up high. I just might have a use, you never know."

I hear his voice trail off down the hall as he leaves, but I make it a point not to look back at him.

I don't need to.

I catch him watching me every time he leaves the room. It's something he does often. I'm not sure why, but it feels like he doesn't want to leave the room without one last glance my way. Every. Time. When he pulls this little move, he makes a point of looking me in the eyes. Because I know the look will always linger, just a little too long, I try to avoid eye contact, and I always preoccupy myself when he's leaving the room, but it doesn't work. I always look up and he always locks eyes with mine.

This time I've preoccupied my time by stepping out to the beautiful outdoor living space that is so vast there are four sets of French doors that lead from the enormous kitchen to where I stand. He's right; it is a fine day, and it's turning into an even finer evening as well.

Before long, the first guests arrive, and with the servers doing most of the work and this being Evelyn's final event with EVC and Mr. McKinley, I stay in the background. I watch her work, and I watch *him* work the room. He is much more personable with his staff outside of the office, and it's clear this sort of get-together is not a first, because he knows the name of each and every spouse and genuinely cares about everyone in the room. He asks about their jobs, children, even pets.

Most importantly, his guests seem at ease around him, and I don't see anyone behaving as if he is the boss and they are his underlings—far from it. He notices me in the background and waves me over.

"Yes, Mr. McKinley, is there something I can get for you?" I ask subtly.

"Olivia, have you had a chance to meet Gloria at the office yet?"

"Yes, sir. We met earlier this week. It's nice to see you again, Mrs. Quinley."

"Nice to see you again, Olivia, but please call me Gloria. No need for formalities," she says, reaching out to shake my hand.

"Gloria's been with my team from the start, and I couldn't do it without her. You'll work with her as often as you will me, so don't hesitate to go to her if I'm not around." He turns his attention to the silver-haired gentleman to her left. "And this is her husband, David. He's got a mean golf game, but I can still take him on the racquet ball court."

His hand touches my shoulder as he continues his introduction, but I barely hear it. His touch has all of my senses on high alert, and I swear I can hear my own blood raging through my veins. "David, this is Olivia. She'll be stepping in to fill some of Evelyn's tasks as well as some additional tasks we're adding to the role."

We continue to make small talk, and he introduces me to his dinner guests. He is professional yet personable. He insists I eat with everyone, and when

Evelyn assures me this is the usual procedure and that no team member is less than the others, I take my seat. I'm used to my place in the background. I would have thought working for such a big company would have me even more in the background, but *he* runs his team much differently than I would have expected.

Of course, he does.

Dinner conversation is fascinating and normal. There isn't any talk of acquisitions and real estate deals. The evening is full of regular conversation filled with laughter and storytelling. I was relieved when the open seat at the table was at the opposite end of the ever-so-gracious host. Having him too close throws me off balance. Being the new kid in town, it's important I'm not caught off guard. I'm busy making mental notes of all the players here tonight for future use, but it's hard...his rich, deep voice makes it so hard to focus.

I do my best to take it all in. I hope if I stay quiet and simply absorb my new surroundings that should do the trick, but *he* won't let me. He finds a way to include me, if even in the smallest ways. From his end of the table he stills manages to fill me in on the background of the stories being told so I have all of the information and can relate to the conversations. He asks if I'm enjoying my wine. He even tells Russell Berry that they'll have to be sure to include me the next time the team uses the suite at Levi's Stadium for a 49er's game.

It's clear he doesn't exclude anyone, but he is making a point to make sure I feel included and a full-fledged member of the team. I'm sure I am reading too much into it, but every time he speaks my name, it feels personal and private. I love the way my name sounds coming from his perfect lips, but it leaves me feeling exposed.

As dinner starts to wrap up, I can't help but rise from my seat and begin to assist the servers with clearing the table. Any way to find a quick escape is what I need right now. I'm feeling too much, and it's causing an edginess to prickle under the surface, and I need a moment to clear my head.

Evelyn touches my hand gently. "Olivia, you don't need to do that. The staff will get it."

"I don't mind. Besides, I ate so much I need to get up and walk around a bit. This will do me some good." I smile down at her.

This isn't a complete lie, I am stuffed, but I also need a break. Everyone here is fantastic, but I am still well out of my league, and I feel more at home with the team members in the kitchen. This fish is out of her water and needs to take a dip in her usual pond and relax for a beat.

I drop off the dishes I gathered on my way to the kitchen and step outside to what is without a doubt my favorite spot in the house. Letting the cool San Francisco air wash over me and relieve the insecure anxiety that was plaguing me every time *his* warm voice filled the room. But most of all when that warmth was aimed in my direction.

*Olivia, get ahold of yourself if you're going to work side by side with this man every day!*

Besides, I'm not interested in him. Not remotely, but as I discover how incorrectly I may have labeled him, I am feeling a little guilty. He is so incredibly different than the man who had the audacity to interview me on a yacht. The man who so easily made me bristle over the phone when I accepted his job proposal. Who would have thought he was a man who worked so many hours he has to have living quarters at the office? A man who knows the names of all of the spouses of his management team and treats them all like family.

"There you are," he says, but is kind enough not to mention the way I startled when his deep voice shook me from my musings about none other than him. "It's pretty great out here, isn't it?"

I slowly turn in the direction of his silky-smooth voice to find him leaning casually against one of the columns on the patio with his hands in his pockets. As he often does, he takes my ability to speak from me for a brief moment in time, and as if he knows I need to adjust to his presence, he gives me the seconds I need to I find myself again.

"I think it's my favorite place in the house," I confess.

"Mine too." He smiles. "So, Evelyn already gave you the tour?" he asks, pushing off of the column and taking two small steps in my direction.

"No, I've only seen the main floor, and I think it's the greatest kitchen I've ever seen, but there is something tranquil out here. It really is lovely."

"I'm glad you like it."

Silence.

Neither of us speaks or moves for that matter.

*Well, this is awkward.*

"Did you need my assistance, sir?" I ask him in the hopes of ending the hellacious moment that has me starting to sweat.

*Does he have moments like this with Evelyn?*

He claps his hands together. "Yes, thank you. I do that from time to time, don't I. Sorry about that." He smiles and tilts his head to the side ever so slightly, and this ridiculously handsome man who exudes such strength and masculinity is suddenly adorable. There is no other way to describe him at this moment.

I hear myself giggle, and there is no erasing the smile on my face. My reaction seems to amuse him, if the smile that grew from adorable to maybe a little cocky tells his story.

"Are you laughing at me, Olivia?"

"I wouldn't dream of it, sir," I say, trying to school my features, but he can hear the smile in my voice.

"You are a sassy little thing, aren't you?" he says nearly under his breath.

My body heats instantly, and I wonder if I've over-stepped. "I'm so sorry, sir. I...I...didn't mean..."

He lifts his hand, asking me to stop talking, but he doesn't look upset. "Don't be sorry. I like it. I find it, and you, refreshing. But we have something bigger than your sass to deal with at the moment. I have a surprise for Evelyn and was hoping you could help me distract her while I get things ready?"

*He finds me refreshing?*
*He thinks I'm sassy, and he likes it?*

"Of course, I can assist. That's what I'm here for."
*Anything to distract me right now!*

"Great, if you could pretend to have some sort of emergency in the kitchen and keep her out of sight for a couple of minutes so I can get the team out front, that should do the trick."

"I love surprises, I'd love to help."

"You love surprises, do you?"

"Let me rephrase that," I correct myself. "I love surprising other people. I hate to be on the receiving end of surprises."

"Duly noted, Miss Adams." He holds his arm out in front of us and ushers me off the beautiful patio and into the kitchen. I follow him to the dining room where some of the guests are still standing and chatting while the others appear to be in the sitting room, enjoying after dinner drinks. This is where we find Evelyn.

We split up and go our separate ways. Joining Gloria and David on the opposite side of the room, he speaks under his breath, preparing them for the surprise. We both watch each other from across the room, and just before he nods his head to give me the all clear to proceed with his plan, he tilts his head again and that tiny smile graces his features one more time.

Just like minutes ago on the patio, this new move of his elicits a giggle out of me, and shaking my head, I take his queue and tap Evelyn on the shoulder.

"Excuse me, Evelyn."

"Yes, dear. Is everything okay?"

"Yes, everything is fine. We just need you in the kitchen if you have a moment?"

She gives her pardon and follows me into the kitchen. Once there, I realize I have no reason to have her back here with me, so I improvise.

"What is it, dear? What can I help you with?" She's glancing around the kitchen, looking for the fire to put out, but of course, comes up short.

Well, I was going to do this at some point tonight, why not now?

"Evelyn, I wanted to have a moment alone to tell you how much I appreciate you taking me under your wing. I know there is no way to ever replace you, but the fact you were kind enough to teach me all that you can will always mean the world to me. I cannot thank you enough."

"Oh, sweet girl, you don't have to thank me. I'll just be sitting at home bored, so if you ever need anything, you just ring me up, and I'll be here if you need me. You're going to do great, though..."

"Excuse me, ladies," Baxter says from the doorway. "Mr. McKinley is asking for you."

Baxter, I have learned this past week, is nearly always around. He calls himself *Mr. McKinley's driver*, but I'm certain this is not his only job title. The two men have a short-hand with each other unlike anything I have seen before. Besides, he is all muscles and far too fit to be a driver. There is clearly more to him than his title.

We follow the large "driver" to the front door, and Evelyn can see that all of the other rooms are now empty, and a genuine worry is starting to cloud her face. "Baxter, what's happened? Why has everyone left?"

"Miss Evelyn, I think the answer you're looking for is right outside." He opens the front door and then steps aside, and she stops short on the front steps.

"What have you done?" I hear her ask, but I can't see anything from where I stand in the entry way.

I can hear his smooth voice coming from the driveway, but I don't know what he's saying. Evelyn takes a few steps down the stairs, and I'm able to sneak up into the doorway to see what the surprise is all about.

Parked below, with a big red bow atop it, is a silver Lexus ES 350. It's now, I can hear the end of the speech being given by tonight's host.

"...And I also thank you not only for the wonderful work you have displayed over the years, but I thank you for being such an important person in my life. You are and will always be family to me..." He then opens his arm to acknowledge the group of people standing with him. "...And to all of us. We hope your retirement will be all you hope for, but we also hope that you miss us terribly."

Everyone in front of her lifts their champagne classes when he shouts, "To Evelyn!"

And the rest of us repeat, "To Evelyn!"

She finishes her trip down the steps and is embraced by her friends. I take advantage of this moment to retreat back into the house. If I didn't find the task of taking her place daunting already, I sure as heck do now.

Back in the kitchen, I find a half-full bottle of champagne and pour myself a glass. I know it's only been a week, but I'm already doubting myself. Things have gone well so far, but Evelyn was by my side. She is so dang good at her job, and so very loved. Forget the job being more than I ever expected, how do you fill the shoes of a woman like her?

I can hear goodbyes being given, and I know I should go up front and say goodbye as well, but instead I feel the pull of the back patio again and take a seat at the big dining table. I think I'll just let Evelyn and Ronan have their time together and let her say goodbye to her friends without her replacement hovering in her shadow. Yes, back here with my half-empty bottle of champagne is just fine with me.

Putting the bottle down on the table after filling my second glass of bubbly, I hear my name being called, and I bolt up from my seat. I don't know why but I feel like a child being caught with my hand in the cookie jar.

Evelyn finds me just as I stand. "There you are. What are you doing back here by yourself?"

I open my mouth to answer when *he* joins us on the patio. "Hiding back here, were you?"

"Not hiding, just giving you all your space." I look the woman of the hour in the eye and admit my truth to her, not caring that *he* will hear it too. "I'll never be able to fill your shoes, and everyone here knows it. No need to have me waiting in the shadows. Besides, it was *your* moment with *your* friends, and I thought I would take a little break back here." Moving my attention to the debonair man now beside her, I say, "I really like it back here." I smile repeating my earlier statement.

Evelyn, tells me not to give it a second thought and Ronan smiles.

"Olivia, I'm going to walk Evelyn out, but if you don't mind staying just a bit longer, I'd like to go over a few things."

"Of course, Mr. McKinley. Whatever you need."

Evelyn, pulls me into a hug and whispers in my ear. "Take good care of him. He can be a handful, but I know if anyone can keep him in line, it's you."

She releases me, leaving me wondering what exactly she means by her last statement, and I almost miss his lingering look over his shoulder when they leave me on my own on the patio.

Expecting to take notes when he returns, I take my phone out and notice a text from Bryce, asking me how the night went. I let him know it's gone well, but that I'm still here. I'm sure he's in bed already, so I don't expect a reply. So far, Bryce seems fine with a daily text, but we've only talked a couple of times.

I can hear Ronan's footsteps in the hallway, and goosebumps start to cover my body in anticipation. I hear him entering the kitchen and then the patio. My body is in overdrive at his mere presence.

"Thank you for staying. You don't mind if I join you, do you?" he asks, holding a champagne flute in his hand as he takes a seat across from me, filling his glass.

"It's your patio and your champagne. Join away."

"There's that sass again."

"Excuse me?"

"So, I think it's important you get to know my properties. You'll want to know what we'll have access to when we need to host an event," he says, ignoring his comment about my sass and getting right to business.

"Yes, that would be great. I'll make it a point of researching them online this weekend." Opening up the notes app on my phone, I ask, "Are there any particular properties that are a priority?"

He clears his throat and takes a drink. "Actually, I was thinking it might be easier if I just take you there myself. Nothing better than researching in person. The Portland deal should be wrapped up by Wednesday. We'll leave Thursday and be back in the office Tuesday, if your weekend is open?"

My thumbs hover over my phone's keyboard.

"I'm sorry, sir. Did you say the weekend?"

"I did. I understand it's your personal time, but I did make it clear there would be travel as a part of the job."

"Yes, yes you did. I'm sorry, I just wasn't expecting a trip so soon, and I still need to find an apartment."

"I've already told you that you can stay at the Saint Francis as long as you need. If you need help looking for a place, don't hesitate to ask."

"No, I'll be fine, but thank you for the offer. I have a couple of places to look at tomorrow, so who knows, I might get lucky. Thursday will be fine either way, though. Would you like me to make arrangements? Any meetings I can set up for you?"

"No, I'll make the arrangements."

"Are you sure? It is my job to take care of these sorts of things. No time like the present for me to take things over," I say nervously, wondering if he doesn't have confidence in my ability to plan a last-minute trip.

"There's plenty of time for that. Let me take care of this trip and the rest are yours from here on out. Deal?"

"Mr. McKinley, if that's what you prefer, then of course, by all means, plan away."

"I'd prefer you call me Ronan, and I'd like to plan the trip. I'll send you any details you'll need as I have them."

"Thank you, sir. Is there anything else you need tonight or shall I call my car?"

"That will be it for the night. You are free to go, Olivia. No need to call a car, though. I'll have Baxter take you back to the hotel. Thank you for all of your hard work this week. Let me go find Baxter for you." We both stand from the table, and he gathers the glasses and now empty bottle of champagne.

Walking ahead of me, his eyes can't hold mine when he leaves the room, thankfully, but he says over his shoulder, "I'll see you on Monday, Miss Adams."

I feel myself starting to panic at the prospect of spending five days with him. I knew travel would be a part of the job, but a trip simply to show me his properties isn't what I expected.

*Game face, Oliva. He never needs to know how he makes you feel. Just keep it together and keep your game face in place.*

## CHAPTER SEVEN

*Ronan*

To say I've been looking forward to today would be an understatement. I know it's irrational. She's my employee, and frankly, I don't think she really even likes me that much, but I still can't wait to show her Haven.

"So, you sure about this trip?" Baxter asks from the front seat.

"And what exactly is that supposed to mean?" I bristle.

"Well, I don't recall you taking time away from the office to spend a long weekend showing Evelyn one of your properties. Just sayin', boss man."

He's right. I know he's right. I also hate that he sees right through me, but who knows me better than him? "It's a business trip, Baxter, and I would thank you kindly if you would leave your nose out of it. If I need security detail or anything else, I'll let you know, old man."

"Don't, *old man*, me. I may be ten years older than you, but I can still take you, Ronan. Name the time and place, my friend."

"Right...I'm going to go rounds with an employee so you can sue me after I beat your saggy ass. I'm smarter than I look, grandpa."

He's only forty-four, and he is in better shape than

most men his age or mine. I'm fit and I have height over him, but even my huge ego can admit he would probably kick my ass. He's my head of security for a reason. He may play the part of my driver, but he is my friend and an intricate part of my team. My security team.

"Watch it. Carly is sixteen now and those grandpa jokes of yours...they aren't funny. At all."

I open my mouth to make another dickhead comment, but my mental faculties come to a complete halt when I see the vision outside my window.

It doesn't surprise me to see her standing in front of the Saint Francis, suitcase at her feet and travel bag over her shoulder. She is a perfectionist and wouldn't dream of keeping me waiting.

In less than two weeks, this fact about her wasn't hard to detect. Always, the first one in the office, excluding myself, and utterly professional and put together at all times.

I don't know what it is about seeing her in a long, flowing summer dress with simple sandals and a jean jacket, but it has me mesmerized. Her dark hair is blowing in the wind, but unfortunately, her eyes are hidden by her big sunglasses.

Before the car has come to a complete stop, I have the door open and am stalking her way. I have two things thundering through me right now. One, I don't want Baxter to help her with her bags. I want to say hello to her first, and I want to be the one to assist her. Two, I don't like the way she was smiling and laughing with the valet while she waited. I have this overwhelming urge to punch the young punk in the face, throw her over my shoulder like a heathen, and toss her in the car, but I resist.

"Good morning, Miss Adams. You look lovely

today." And just like that my comment has caused her back to go ram-rod stiff, and her demeanor has changed from fun and care-free with valet-boy, to polite and uptight with me. Part of me hates getting this reaction from her, but the other part of me is thrilled whenever I get a reaction of any kind from her.

A good morning in return is her only reply, and when valet-boy attempts to take her bags to the car, I stop him, tip him, and send him on his way. I load her bags into the trunk of the car, and when I shut it, I see Baxter standing next to the driver's side door with a shit-eating grin on his face. He knows me too damn well.

If Olivia wasn't standing between us, I might tell him exactly what he can do with his smile, but she is standing there, looking gorgeous as ever. But deep down, I don't give a good God damn what he or anyone else thinks. My need to be near her overpowers everything else.

I open the door to the car for her, and she slides in silently. I have a feeling getting her to loosen up this weekend isn't going to be easy. But whoever said life was easy? I like a challenge, and this woman has been that since the moment she stepped onto my boat in Portland.

I try to make small talk, but she isn't much of a participant. Having her next to me with only the small space between us on the back seat feels awkward for her, this much is obvious. For me, there is a pull between us. A pull that is screaming that the most natural thing to do right now would be to take her hand in mine. I have a feeling there would be a resignation letter on my desk within the hour if I acted on that desire.

I can't take the reserved conversation, so I begin telling her about Haven. When I start describing the resort to her, she comes to attention, and I can see her taking mental notes of everything I say.

"There isn't going to be a test, Olivia. I just want you to experience Haven for yourself and get a feel for our properties. It's a pretty special place, and I hope you like it."

"I look forward to seeing it. I can't wait to see the meeting spaces and ballrooms in person. It's so much easier to plan an event if you've actually been in the space."

"Exactly the point of the trip, Miss Adams," I lie like a dog. Baxter clears his throat to get my attention and to let me know that the party in the front seat calls bullshit on my reasoning.

She is finally loosening up when we pull onto the tarmac at the airport. When Baxter parks the car in front of the private EVC plane, she shakes her head ever so slightly, and a small grin plays at her lips.

"Do I dare ask what you're thinking right now, Miss Adams?"

"You can dare to ask if you please, sir, but I wouldn't suggest it." She opens her door herself, stepping onto the tarmac and then closes the door leaving me inside.

Sass.

She is full of it, and it leaves me feeling confused, amused, and hard as hell.

One minute she is uptight and professional, and the next she is giving me sass like nobody's business. I feel like I've got whiplash, but the car isn't even in motion. I have to admit, I like it. It adds to the challenge that is Olivia Adams.

Baxter beats me to the trunk this time and is handing our bags to the crew of the plane when I join him at the back of the car. Olivia is standing patiently with her bag over her shoulder, and her hair is blowing in the breeze once again.

"You don't stand a chance with a girl like her. You're a goner, my friend." Baxter speaks the truth, but it doesn't mean I need him to share his every thought about the situation with me. His smart-ass comments aren't helping me at all.

"Keep it to yourself, if you don't mind?" This is the best I've got at the moment. She throws me off my game, and I don't have enough wits about me to fight back right now.

Watching her board the plane ahead of me, I can hear her words from our meeting in Portland. *Less is more.* As she takes in the tan leather seats and the plush surroundings of the plane, I hear it over and over in my head. *Less is more.* I feel a bit of embarrassment at the opulence of the plane, but her disapproval is adorable.

Shrugging out of my leather jacket, I make sure I'm watching her face when I say, "The flight is only an hour and a half, but if you need to lie down, there is a bedroom in the back. Feel free."

The roll of her eyes and the complete irritation on her face is exactly what I was hoping for. I can't help but chuckle as I get myself situated and Gretchen, our flight attendant, brings me orange juice and a copy of the *Wall Street Journal*.

When she asks Olivia what she'd like, I see her read her name tag before she replies, "Thank you, Gretchen. A bottle of water would be great."

When Gretchen steps aside, Stew, the Captain of the plane, introduces himself to her and when she replies by calling him by his first name, she makes a point to look in my direction as if to make sure that I've noticed she called both of them by their first names.

She's not very subtle, is she?

I can't help but laugh out loud at her sass, and when I do, I see another ghost of a smile light up her eyes. She looks away and pulls out her tablet and starts reading. She reads through the rest of the flight and doesn't look my way even once. I'd love to know what the hell she's reading, but I'm afraid if it were anything other than a dirty romance novel, I would be dreadfully disappointed.

When we land in Orange County, there is a car waiting for us. We pack up quickly and are on the road in minutes. She watches out the window and stays quiet on the drive to the marina.

When we arrive, she looks confused, but she finally speaks and out comes the sass I am growing very fond of.

"Another yacht? Really?" She scrunches up her nose, speaking under her breath, almost to herself.

When I say, "Not a yacht, just a small speedboat to get us to the island," she gasps and covers her mouth with her hand.

"I am so sorry, Mr. McKinley. I didn't mean to say that out loud." When she sees the smile on my face, she loosens up and smiles herself. "I am glad to hear it's not another luxurious form of transportation. I've had enough for one day."

"Well, you may be disappointed. The speedboat may be a bit more luxurious than you are expecting."

"I'm coming to expect no less from you, sir."

Olivia Adams is something else.

Walking down the marina, I see Lou in the distance where he waits for us next to one of my favorite toys, my *Rivarama*. The mahogany deck and cream benches and chairs stand out amongst the rest, and I love her so. Yes, she is a speed boat, but she is forty-four feet long and can seat ten. There is a bedroom and bathroom below as well as a saloon. She is one of my pride and joys.

I greet Lou and help him load our bags onto the boat. I offer my hand to Olivia, and as I help her into the boat, she makes a tisking sound and shakes her head.

"Some speed boat, Mr. McKinley," she says, taking my hand.

"You don't approve, Miss Adams?" I say, hating that she's let go of my hand now that she is safely aboard.

"She's beautiful, sir. But, you know...less is more and all that."

And there it is. I knew that was what she was thinking on the plane. She may be sassy, but she never disappoints. I barely know her, but I already know what she's thinking, and I like it.

"We'll see what you say after you've gone for a ride. Give her a chance, and I think she may just change your mind." She doesn't comment as I walk past her. "Make yourself comfortable, we'll be off in just a minute."

Lou and I discuss the water conditions, and I push the button that brings the beautiful vessel to life. We pull the boat away from the marina, and *The Jupiter* parked next to her, and slowly bring her to full speed. I love this feeling. It's only here on the water or on my motorcycle that I feel free, and all of the usual pressures of life seems to fade away.

I look over my shoulder to see how she's doing with the speed, and I'd say my sweet *Rivarama* may be changing someone's mind. I told her to get comfortable, and that is exactly what she did. Her feet are up, and her head is back with her hair whipping around her happy face. She isn't grinning from ear to ear, but she looks relaxed, and there is a small smile on her face that says it all.

She feels free too.
The water. The wind. The quiet.
There is something to be said for it.

The feel of the wind on your face, the spray from the water cooling your skin, and the roar of the boat speeding through the water. It's loud and intense, blocking out all other sound until you only hear the hum of the boat and the splash of the water. It's the loudest quiet you'll ever experience, in the best way possible.

There is nothing like it.

I can see her experiencing it all on her face. Her glasses are still on, but I know her eyes are closed. She is relaxed and loving every second of it. I'm glad I can bring her this small moment of peace. I tear my gaze from her and focus on the water ahead.

A short time later, we pull up to the Catalina Island marina. Lou jumps out to grab the rope and tie us in while I finish parking the boat. Olivia is running her fingers through her hair, trying to calm the knotted mess that comes along with the freedom of the water, and I can tell she feels like a mess too. I wish I could tell her how beautiful she looks, but she doesn't take to my compliments too terribly well, so I'll keep it to myself.

We leave the boat behind and find a car waiting for us. We're in another back seat together, but this time she makes conversation.

"Mr. McKinley, as much as it pains me to say it, you were right. She did win me over. I could have stayed out on the water all day. That was amazing." She says this looking out the car window and not to my face. I think it was hard for her to admit.

"Miss Adams, I am not sorry to say that your pain brings me pleasure and satisfaction. I knew she would win you over. I also know it was hard for you to admit you were wrong, so please know I appreciate your confession."

She rolls her eyes, but this time she turns to face me. "How is it possible that you seem to make everything sound so inappropriate? You have a real gift for it, you know that?" She follows this with a giggle I haven't heard before.

It pleases me she took my words the way she did. She's not a pure and gentle little girl who lets things slip past her. She calls me out on my bullshit, and it's hot as hell.

*She is your employee.*

As we near the hotel, I'm starting to feel anxious, not a feeling I'm used to. I work on high pressure deals with international companies, and I don't generally get as nervous as I am right now. I have a great deal of pride in all of my properties, but this one in particular. I have a special place in my heart for Haven, and some part of me is seeking her approval. She has a look of glee on her face when she gets out of the car. She takes in the beauty of the hotel and spins in a little circle as she takes in the open and ornate ceilings in the front entrance.

*She does love a good ceiling. This is a good start, McKinley.*

"Your bags will be taken to your suite. Would you like to take a walk around the grounds now, and then you can take a little break before dinner?"

"Yes, please," she says sounding giddy. "I can't wait to see the event space."

Once we're discussing work, she is back to professional, and the glee from before has gone and changed to serious and professional. I've shown her the ballrooms, meeting rooms, and restaurants. She hasn't said much, but she has taken some notes on her tablet.

When we enter the outdoor event space, often home to weddings, she lifts her sunglasses to the top of her head and her face lights up. "Oh, Mr. McKinley...everything about Haven is beautiful, but this space...it's simply breathtaking. This view of the water and the trees and all the flowers. I can't even imagine what it looks like at sunset. And these gardens..."

*You, are simply breathtaking...*

I've stopped on the path to the gardens while she continues to walk ahead of me, and I watch her as she takes in my favorite place on the property. The gardens at Haven are breathtaking, she's right about that. Olivia Adams standing in the center of the space takes the beauty around us to a whole new level. The back patio at Francis Street was her favorite place in my house, and now it appears the gardens are her favorite place at Haven.

*Duly noted.*

She is floating around the garden paths and beaming with excitement. I swear her smile must be blinding the sun.

"Whoever designed this space has a perfect eye and attention to detail."

I don't know why I don't tell her it was me. This was a dream of mine brought to life, and I couldn't be filled with more pride, knowing she loves the space. It's enough.

"I'm glad you like it."

"Like it, I love it! I bet you have a waiting list a mile long of couples who want to get married here."

"We do, but we try to limit the number of events

we do. We like them to be special, and we want to be sure that our other guests that come here for the beautiful surroundings also get to enjoy the space. If there was a wedding here every weekend, it would make it hard to make that happen."

"Of course. A wedding at Haven should be unique. Special. It's brilliant."

"See, we're on the same page. I told you we would work well together."

"We shall see. It's still early in the day." She says this with a smile but pulls her sunglasses back in place, covering her eyes. It's probably a good thing. I find it damn hard to concentrate when I'm around her, but when she looks me in the eye, not much gets accomplished.

"Yes, it is. And on that note, let me show you to your room. I'm sure you could use a break from your tyrant of a boss."

She replies with an eye roll and says, "You could say that again." This time she smiles shyly as if she almost doesn't mean for her sass to slip out.

When we walk back through the lobby to the elevator, she asks questions all along the way. She is genuinely interested in the property and wants to know everything she can about the resort. We reach her floor, and I step out with her and walk her to her room. When I pull her room key out of my pocket, she seems a little surprised, but I ignore her expression and open the door.

"I hope you'll find everything to your liking. It looks like the team has dropped off your bags. Is there anything else I can get you?"

What I really mean is, is there anything I can do to stay here with you just a little while longer? Even when she's quiet and professional, I still enjoy being near her. The energy between the two of us is intoxicating.

And I'm always waiting to see when the next little piece of sass is going to appear. I find myself looking forward to those moments more than I should.

"Thank you, Mr. McKinley. The room is perfect and I will be just fine." She takes a few steps toward the window. "This view is breathtaking, and with this little patio to sit on and relax, I'm not sure what else I could ask for. I have everything I need."

This time she is glowing when she looks back and takes in the rest of her room. I try my best not to puff my chest out with pride.

"Well, if you're sure, then I'll leave you to it and give you a few hours to settle before we meet for dinner. We didn't really have much of a lunch, so I called ahead and made sure you had fruit, cheese, and some other things to snack on before dinner."

"Thank you, that was very kind of you, sir."

My hand is on the door, and there is no reason left for me to stay. It's time to go.

"I'll see you at dinner then."

She nods and her lack of conversation tells me she's ready for me to take my leave. Once in the hall, I take the stairs up the one floor to the Penthouse, and I can't help but think to myself how else I can continue to impress her and, more importantly, continue to bring that smile to her gorgeous face.

Once in my room, I call the concierge and set the rest of the evening in motion. "Mr. Cross, good afternoon..."

## CHAPTER EIGHT

*Olivia*

I disconnect my call with Bryce, feeling like I've just hung up with the utility company instead of my boyfriend. I'm surprised he didn't ask me if I wanted to take a survey to rate my satisfaction with our call before we hung up. Our calls, as always, feel transactional and forced. I know it's wrong, but I don't feel anything close to what I felt ten minutes ago when I received a text from my new boss.

A simple text telling me what time dinner would be and to wear a cocktail dress was all it took for my heart to flutter like it never has before.

I've always known Bryce wasn't *the one*, but he is easy, and we don't need anything from each other, other than occasional companionship. As far as science nerds go, he's pretty hot, but he isn't very sexual. Our sex is *also* somewhat transactional, and sometimes I feel like he would rather be working than actually be in the moment with me when we are in bed.

I know I could have ended it long ago, and I have had other offers, but the thought of meeting someone new or losing the safe stability of being with Bryce has been reason enough for me to stick with it. It would be nice to be desired, but I've spent so much of my life with a small level of fear always just under the surface, looking over my shoulder and simply trying to get through life day by day, that worrying about a relationship and the complications that come with it, isn't something I'm interested in.

What I am interested in, is this amazing hotel I'm lucky enough to be staying at. The idea that maybe one day I will get to plan an event here myself is pretty exciting! As beautiful as my room is, I can't wait to check out more of the property. I know it's early and dinner isn't for quite some time, but I can't help it. I'm going to get ready now and then take a nice stroll in the gardens and see what visions for future events come to mind.

I bop along to the music coming from my phone while I take my shower and get ready. I spend a little extra time on my hair and make-up, all the while telling myself that I'm not doing it for *him*. Nope, that would just be silly. He's my boss and that's all.

Taking a look at the clothes hanging in my hotel closet, I know my clothes aren't really up to the standards of the designer suits my boss wears, but working in the event industry means I have lots of subtle, little, black, cocktail dresses, but I'd say I'm due for a few new items. After I get my first paycheck and find an apartment, I have to make sure I take myself shopping. I know I have a lot of student loan debt to pay down, but moving to EVC has given me quite the pay raise, and I've earned a day of splurging!

What I have with me will do, so I grab my favorite little, black dress and leisurely stroll into the bathroom. I really could sit on my balcony all day and stare at the view or read a good book, but I didn't go on my run this morning so a walk around the property will do me some good. I usually feel a little jittery if I haven't exercised. It clears my head and keeps me balanced. It's very rare when I take a day off. A walk around Haven isn't a five-mile jog, but it will still do me some good.

I slip on my dress and heels and grab my clutch and phone. I may or may not check for another text from *him*, but of course there isn't one. I am the employee and not somebody he texts for non-work-related topics. I sure wouldn't mind the rush of excitement I had when I received his earlier text, though. A girl could develop a minor addiction to feeling so giddy.

I leave my room and take in my surroundings as I go. Haven is extravagant but in a comfortable way. A person of my standing can appreciate the luxuries and the details but still not feel as though they are out of their element. It is breathtakingly beautiful with a feeling of comfort. It's warm, that's what it is. Warm and inviting.

I arrive on the ground floor and slowly follow the route we took earlier today and find myself back in the gardens. The gardens are lush and filled with flowers of all different colors, sizes, and fragrances. My favorites are the Catalina Island Flowers that Mr. McKinley showed me early today. I thought the white ones were my favorites, but now that I've found the vibrant pink ones, they may be taking the top spot.

I follow the garden path to the open green space that ends with the jeweled sapphire of the ocean, and I am truly mesmerized. It's quiet and tranquil, and I cannot wait to plan my first wedding here! My mind is flooded with ideas, and I take my phone out to make some notes so I don't forget. Looking down, I find a pink Catalina Island Flower and figure, what the heck, and put the flower behind my ear.

When I look up to get another glance at the white gazebo that just screams romance, I see the staff has started to set up a table for two. The table is topped with white linens, and a bouquet of my new favorite flower, only in white, adorns the table along with white candles. Small white lights have been turned on, and if I was a betting woman, I would say there may be a ring in a tiny box that just might be given to one lucky person in that gazebo tonight. If I'm right, then kudos to the person who planned this romantic meal, because I know I would certainly say, yes! I mean, it doesn't get much more romantic. Or maybe it's an anniversary celebration for a couple that was married here years ago?

I check the time on my phone and realize I need to be in the lobby bar to meet *him* for dinner in a few minutes, so I turn back down the garden path toward the hotel. I kind of wish I was staying to see who the lucky couple was going to be.

Feeling exhilarated at the thought of my future planning events here and at other EVC properties, I feel an extra little spring in my step when I enter the lobby bar where we're supposed to meet. As usual, when I see him waiting for me, that spring in my step turns into a small stutter-step and there goes my dang balance again.

The moment I enter the bar, I can feel his stare, and directly in front of me sits the classically handsome man who makes me feel more than I should. Even if I am the only one who knows, it's still embarrassing. And cliché. Having a crush on the hot, wealthy boss is so very typical, and I always pride myself on being anything but typical.

His gaze has me in his grip from across the room, and he isn't letting me go. What is happening and what planet am I on that a man like him would be looking at *me* like he is? I know he does that eye contact thing at the office, but this is even more intense, if that is even possible?

Rising from his seat as I approach the table, he is pure perfection. As I often do at the office when I watch his charm politely bend someone to his will, I can't help but hum the song *Classic Man* in my head when I take him in. His expertly tailored suit, sans tie, a look he wears so well, is draped across what I can only assume is a perfect body underneath it. Flawless dark hair, impeccable complexion, and eyes as blue as the water playing center stage in my view on the edge of the Haven gardens.

"Olivia, it's nice to see you again." He leans down and kisses my cheek as his hand gently rests on my hip. "You look lovely this evening."

*This isn't a date. Right?*

I find myself looking over my shoulder like I may be in the wrong place, but the man stepping away from my scalding hot cheek and hip is in fact my employer. Yep, I'm in the right place.

*Olivia Adams, he is your boss. He is a sophisticated man, and this is how he greets women. He probably greets his mother the same way.*

"Hello, Mr. McKinley," I say shakily while I take my seat.

"Olivia," he sighs. "Please call me Ronan. You are going to spend more time with me than you would probably like, so we may as well get to know each other and at least call each other by our first names."

I'm not sure why I still can't say his first name. Maybe because it feels too intimate or because of the way my "interview" on the boat felt. I don't want him to ever get the impression that there is more than a working relationship between us.

Or maybe it's me I'm trying to convince?

Or I'm more stubborn than I thought.

He stands next to my chair with his hands in his pockets and tilts his head to the side. He looks like he's struggling to figure me out. I wish he would just sit down and stop trying.

Finally, he takes the seat across from me, and it doesn't help because now he's…right…there. "So, what can I get for you? Would you like a glass of wine?"

*God, yes, I need a drink!*

"A glass of white would be nice, thank you."

He lifts his finger and gains the attention of our server and orders my wine.

"So, *Olivia*, did you find your room to your liking?"

"I did, thank you. I also took another little stroll around the property, and I just can't stay away from the gardens. They're beautiful. I think the dark pink Catalina Island Flowers are my new fave."

"I see that," he says with a nod toward me.

I was so taken aback by his presence I forgot I had slipped the flower behind my ear. I nervously make sure the adornment is still securely in place and carry on.

"I have a million ideas for different events to have here. I have to say, I think I could just work here and spend my days in that garden, and I would be perfectly happy."

The corners of his mouth slowly rise into a smile that would make you think he planted the gardens himself. He's beaming with pride.

"I'm glad to hear it," he says as he nods his head to someone behind me. "If you're ready, it appears our table is ready."

He stands and helps pull my chair out while I stand. He guides me out the back door I just came through and in the direction of the gardens.

The sun is slowly beginning it's decent over the water, and the pink tint in the sky only adds to the beauty and elegance that surrounds us. I follow his lead and stroll leisurely amongst the flowers and enjoy the tranquility and quiet.

I'm so in the moment that it takes me a few seconds after we've left the gardens to realize we're headed for the candlelit gazebo. A few feet away, I finally find my voice.

"That's not for us."

"Oh, but it is, Miss Adams."

"Sir, what is this?"

"Dinner."

"Here?"

"Well, yes. Do you have a problem with the table? After seeing your enthusiasm for the gardens earlier today, I thought you might like to have dinner here. Was I wrong?"

"Yes!" I hiss on a whisper.

"Excuse me, you don't like the gardens?" He has the gall to sound perplexed.

"Well, no, of course I do. But this is a romantic, candlelit dinner. People passing by would most certainly think we were a couple on a date. It just feels a little, I don't know, inappropriate."

I'm starting to perspire—not the first time my body has reacted like this because of this man—and I can feel the heat of my blush covering my face. But I'm starting to feel extremely uncomfortable. Is this the real reason he hired me? Are all of my worst nightmares coming true? All the feelings I was having on that yacht just weeks ago are flooding back, and I can feel my anger building at a steady pace.

"Well, I am very sorry if my plans have offended

you. This was never my attention. I simply thought you might like to experience the setting you'll be planning in."

"Is that so?"

"Ha," he huffs a laugh at me. "Yes, Olivia. Many of our clients that get married here do so at sunset and the gazebo has a front row view."

He grabs my hand and pulls us toward the stairs. I resist and pull back, but he doesn't let me go and pulls me up the first step.

"Do you always make everything so difficult?" He says under his breath.

*What the hell?*

I notice the server standing to the left of the gazebo with all of their preparations, and I feel bad that I'm causing a scene. I rip my hand from his and finish taking the remaining three steps to the table.

He pulls a chair out and with a surly voice says, "Sit."

Feeling a little petulant, I plop myself down into my seat and gulp the remainder of wine and loudly set down the empty glass. He takes his seat, lifting a bottle of wine out of the ice bucket next to the table and refills my glass with the same wine I was drinking inside.

Within moments, some other resort guests walk by, and I can hear the woman sigh with envy. I can't help but let out a little giggle at the thought of anyone thinking we could be a couple, and let's face it, they've proven my point. We do, in fact, look like a couple.

He hears my giggle and lifts one arrogant eyebrow in reply. He knows they've proven me right, and he knows it makes me uncomfortable, and it brings him some kind of twisted joy. I take another sip of my wine and let him relish his moment.

Making me uncomfortable seems to be his favorite pastime. Between the stares over his shoulder when he leaves a room and insisting I call him by his first name to his over-the-top yacht, private plane, and now a candlelit dinner at sunset with me, his employee.

"So, I thought since we're going to be working and traveling together we should get to know each other. Tell me a little about yourself, Olivia."

*Oh, good gracious. Are we going to start braiding each other's hair too? There will be no dark secrets shared in this gazebo.*

"There isn't really much to tell. I'm pretty boring."

He narrows his eyes, and looking resolute, says, "I seriously doubt that."

"Well, you would be seriously wrong, Mr. McKinley."

He chuckles and we both take a drink of our wine, but we hold each other's gaze. It's almost as if there is an unspoken competition and neither of us wants to look away first. It appears we are both equally stubborn.

The only thing that breaks our showdown is the server bringing our first course to the table. The first course being a cream of roasted celery and horseradish soup with citrus crème fraîche. He drops off our food and leaves us alone again.

"I thought we would have the chef set up a tasting menu for us so you could get a sample of what we offer. I hope you don't mind."

"Not at all. That's a great idea, thank you."

We eat our soup, and things grow quiet again. But I'm not foolish enough to think this respite will last. And just as I have this thought, he speaks again.

"Where did you grow up?"

*Here we go.* "We moved around a bit. We were

here and there."

"Are you close to your parents?"

*Please don't go there.* "No."

*Why does he need to get personal?*

*How does this help our working relationship?*

"Would you like to be?"

"Of course, Mr. McKinley. Who doesn't want to be?"

"Where in the world would you like to go?"

*Is he filling out my dating profile right now?* "Sir, this feels like we're on a date, and I'm not sure it feels appropriate."

He clears his throat and looks sincere. "I am very sorry if my questions are making you uncomfortable. I meant it when I said the two of us are going to be spending a lot of time together. I really did think it was a good idea to get to know each other."

For the first time, he looks uneasy. I can tell that I've now made him feel uncomfortable, and I feel a little bad. I know I'm being uptight about not saying his name or really getting to know him. I've been so set on knowing I was hired for my ability to do the job and for no other reason.

"I'm the one who's sorry. I'm trying too hard to be professional and prove to you you've hired the right person that I may be making things harder than they need to be. I can't help but feel we look like a couple sitting here at a candlelit table for two. You aren't asking inappropriate questions, I'm just a bit on edge. I can't help but imagine what my boyfriend would think if he saw us."

He stills and doesn't respond for a few seconds.

"Do you want to go inside?"

"Not at all. This is absolutely beautiful. It just

feels a little intimate is all."

"So, a boyfriend then?"

My cheeks blush as the conversation turns even more personal, but I don't reply.

"Is it serious?"

"Yes."

"Do you live together?"

"No. We've talked about it the last couple of years, but no."

"Two years?" he sputters out when he chokes on his wine.

"Well, we've been together for three, but we aren't in any rush?"

His brows furrow, and he sits back casually in his chair. "How will he feel about you traveling?"

"He won't mind. We aren't joined at the hip or anything. He understands and besides, his work keeps him busy."

"Is that right?"

The confident man is back, and his arrogance is once again shining through.

Our next course of scallops wrapped in salmon, wasabi jelly, and a sweet pomegranate is delivered, and the subject changes to the delicious food. This is all a bit fancier than I am accustomed to, but in the world of event planning, you do get exposed to many dishes most aren't lucky enough to try. It may not be the way I usually eat, but that doesn't mean I don't enjoy tasting the finer things in life at work.

As the courses continue to arrive, our conversation has turned back to work and menu items that could go with certain events and themes.

After dessert, he insists we walk our meal off. Not much is said during our short stroll that brings us back to the entrance of the resort and the lobby bar. Our walk has been comfortable, and I find myself enjoying his company. He's pleasant, smart, and engaging. There is a magnetism about him that draws you in even when walking in complete silence.

"Would you like a nightcap?"

*And, it feels like a date again.*

"Thank you, sir, but I'm tired and plan on getting an early start tomorrow. Thank you for the offer, though."

Walking me to the elevator, he keeps his hands in his pockets and then we wait, once more in silence, until the doors open. I enter the elevator, and when I turn back and wait for the doors to close, he holds his position and watches me with his crystal blue eyes and a look of determination—what he's determined of, I have no idea.

The doors close, and I feel myself sag against the back wall of the elevator. I hadn't realized how hard I was trying to keep the upper hand and stay professional. I really am exhausted. Exhausted from fighting the way he makes me feel and telling myself I don't want him.

*I shouldn't have taken this job.*

These six words run on a loop in my head while I slowly step onto my floor once my short ride in the elevator is over. I take my time getting my key card out, unlocking the door, and entering my dark room. I find the switch on the wall, and to see the room glow in the low light makes it even more beautiful than it was earlier in the day.

Still, at a snail's pace, I walk through the room tossing my key and clutch onto the desk in the living space. I don't understand what I'm feeling. To say the least, I'm confused. I couldn't get away from *him* fast enough, but I'm still wishing I was with him. I'm finding that I enjoy being in his presence. Even though I know he's my boss and nothing can come of it, I love to simply be near him.

Come to think of it...when I wake up every morning excited to go to work, it isn't my desk I see when I open my eyes each day, it's *him*.

I sigh heavily and take off my shoes and hang up my dress. I take out my contacts, wash my face, and get ready for bed. Hoping to take my mind off my unprofessional thoughts, I take a seat at the desk and call Bryce.

"Olivia?"

"Hey."

"What's up? Is something wrong?"

"Nope, I just wanted to call."

"Wow, twice in one night. This is new."

"Sorry, am I bugging you?"

"Well, I'm at the lab, but I can take a break."

"Whatcha working on?"

That was a huge mistake. I should have known better. Once he starts talking about work, it's over. As per usual, he gets so worked up about work he ends the call so he can get back to it.

Well, that plan backfired. All that phone call did was make me wonder what I'm doing with him? Our relationship is boring. Safe. Easy. Lifeless. If you combined all of the feelings and emotions I have felt in the years I've known Bryce, they wouldn't come close to adding up to what I feel every time I'm near *him*. Hear *his* voice. Or just know I'm going to spend time with him.

*I shouldn't have taken this job.*

I pour myself a glass of wine and take myself out to the balcony and curl up on one of the loungers that overlooks the dark water. There are lights sparkling on the invisible landscape in the distance, but the stars are center stage on this perfectly clear night.

I think back to the day I mentioned to Alex that Bryce and I were thinking of moving in together, and she asked me if I loved him, because if I didn't we would just be roommates with benefits and that I shouldn't rush into things. She was right. It would have just been a roommate situation.

I silently send her a telepathic thank you. I might not be sitting here on this beautiful balcony, on this beautiful island if I had moved in with Bryce. I think I would have been just as alone as I was in my apartment back in Portland even if I was living with him. I've always used the excuse that I like to be alone, but maybe that's a defensive mechanism. I try not to ever get too close. That way it doesn't hurt if somebody doesn't have time to spend with me. I like to be alone anyway, right?

Then why don't I want to be alone right now. Why have I noticed my solitude more and more every night when I leave the office? Is it because I'm staying in a hotel at the moment? Is it because I'm in a new city? Or because I feel myself waking up more and more every day. Finding myself and feeling energized about life. There is a lot to do in this big world and a lot of interesting people to spend my time with as well.

I regret all the times I've turned down invitations to spend time with Alex and her friends back home, or any of the other girls at work. Alex and I had a standing happy hour date each week, and I did spend time with her and her friends occasionally, but I always find myself pulling back. I don't want to have to share my story. I hate those get-to-know-you questions people always ask and the energy it takes to find vague ways to answer them.

I met Alex in group therapy, so she knows my story. She also knows how I feel about sharing my past, and she does a good job of changing the subject for me, but I don't want to be work for her. She always tells me I only have to share what I want to share and that I have nothing to be afraid of. I've made it through to the other side and put myself through school and I've done it all on my own.

She's right. I am proud of myself, but I still don't feel the need to share my story. There isn't anyone else I have ever felt close enough to. Bryce knows some of my story, but I'm not sure he ever really hears what I'm saying. When I say more than a sentence or two at a time, I can see his face glaze over.

I take a sip of my wine, and it reminds me of my evening with the tall, dark, and handsome man who sat across the candlelit dinner and how hard he was trying to get to know me. He probably asked more personal questions tonight than Bryce has asked me in the last six months.

The memory of his smile at the mention of my adoration for the gardens, or how frustrated he got with me when I refused to take the steps of the gazebo followed by his demand that I sit has me throwing my head back on my lounger and gently stomping my feet. I feel giddy and light.

Happy.

# CHAPTER NINE

*Ronan*

I hate that I only got to see her at breakfast where she was busy laying out my schedule for the day. When she told me about her plans to explore the island alone, I was flooded with anxiety, and all I wanted to do was cancel everything on today's to-do list and go with her.

Not only did I hate the thought of her off on her own in a new place, but I desperately wanted to spend the day with her. This woman, who won't even call me by my first name, has taken over every thought in my head. Not ideal when trying to run a business and trying to woo potential investors.

All I wanted to do was tell her she had to stay and assist me with my meetings and business lunch here at Haven, but it was hard enough to work with just the thought of her in my head let alone having her near me and in plain sight. This morning, watching her talk and not being able to reach out and touch her was almost painful.

She calls to me like nobody ever has, and I'm not quite sure what to do about that.

*She is my employee.*
*She has a boyfriend.*
*Keep it professional, Ronan.*

Out the window is where all my internal reminders go when I watch her bounce into the bar where she's meeting me before dinner. Seeing her in her white, sexy yet sweet, Audrey Hepburn-inspired dress, which is covered in a pattern of flowers, and her face lit up like it is, is worth the time apart. I can't help but smile while I watch her search for me. When she finally sees me, she pauses for a beat, and her hands glide over her dress as she straightens herself and seems to be forcing herself to contain her current level of joy. Just like every time she sees me, her professional side has kicked into gear.

I stand and she stops in front of me, seeming unsure of what to say or do. I take advantage of the moment and lean forward and kiss her cheek. I do my best not to linger but being this close to her is intoxicating. Her floral scent matches her happy dress and the mood she was in before she saw me. I force myself to step away from her, and she takes the seat in the booth across from me.

I didn't pick the dark booth in the corner on purpose. At least that is what I keep telling myself.

"Olivia, if the bounce in your step when you walked in here was any indication, you seem to have had a good day."

"Oh, I did, Mr. McKinley. I love it here!" She says beaming ear to ear. She somehow keeps her smile in place while taking a sip of her water.

"Ronan. Please all me Ronan, Olivia."

I don't mean to sound so stern, but this woman is making me crazy. I just want her to feel comfortable enough to say my damn name! Is that too much to ask? She sits up a bit straighter but crosses her arms in front of her and seems to close off just a bit.

"Tell me how your day went. Where did your

adventures take you today?" I ask, trying to loosen her back up, and this seems to do the trick.

"Well, I actually rented a bike and rode all over Two Harbors. It was adorable and had a little basket in the front with a bell and everything. It was classic." She beams as her arms uncross, and her posture loosens again.

"Rented a bike, did you?"

"I did. I hadn't ridden one since I was tiny, but after a bit, it came back to me. It was a little shaky at first; I'm not gonna lie."

She giggles.

The sound is poetry.

"I would have liked to have seen that."

Her giggle falters, and she locks eyes on mine. For a brief moment, there is something there. But she ends the exchange quickly.

"Well, I wasn't a kid who spent a ton of time riding bikes so I didn't have as much muscle memory to work with. No skinned knees, though. It all worked out just fine. I had such a great day."

*Why did your childhood not include time riding bikes?*

Why do I get a feeling I won't like the answer to my unspoken question?

"So, where did all of this bike riding take you?"

"Everywhere! I just rode and stopped from time to time to admire the view. I took a break at Harbor Sands for lunch and had some mahi-mahi tacos and chips and salsa. It was so good that I just had to have a Pacifico to go along with it. With my feet in the sand and beer in my hand, it almost felt like I was on a tropical vacation."

"Pacifico, huh?"

"Yep, I've never been to Mexico but when your

feet are in the sand and you're eating Mexican food, you just have to throw in the Mexican beer. It's enough for me. I'll get to Mexico one day, and then I'll do it for real. Can't wait."

I find myself making a mental note to find a reason to go to Cabo. Oh, the places I want to take this woman. All she has to do is name the destination, and I'll take her.

"Sounds like you had a better day than I did."

Her eyes go wide with worry. "Oh no, did your meeting with the investors not go well?"

It feels good to see she cares enough to worry about my meetings going well or not. "No, they were productive, and I think they're in, but your day sounds like a lot more fun." My suit jacket pocket vibrates with the text letting me know the car is ready.

"The car is here if you're ready for dinner?" I ask her. It's a good thing because I could honestly sit right here, in this booth, listening to her talk about her day all night long. I think she would rather go to dinner.

"Sure, where are we off to?" she says, grabbing her clutch and sliding out of the booth. We stand at the same moment, and it feels good to see her excited to share a meal with me, unlike last night when she was not only hesitant, but I thought at one point she might just turn and walk away.

———

Our server takes our menus. I make a mental note that she likes halibut and take it upon myself to order her the perfect Chardonnay to go with her meal. She doesn't seem to mind, and in fact, she has been much more relaxed tonight. She talked all the way to the restaurant and continued to tell me about her day and how she can't wait to come back and stay in one of the camping cabins in Two Harbors. Her day of bike riding and exploring not only added a new glow to her naturally tan skin but seems to have done her some good mentally.

Now, if she would relax enough to call me by my name.

"It's nice to see the other side of the island. Who knew there was so much to see? I'm not sure what I pictured, but I love it."

"I'm sorry you were on your own today."

"It's okay; I don't mind. I prefer it most of the time," she says as her gaze turns to the window and the view outside.

"And why is that?"

Quietly she replies, "When you grow up like I did, being alone is often preferable."

She turns red, and I feel an underlying anger begin to stir inside me at the mere implication she may have had anything other than a stellar childhood.

"Why is that, Olivia?"

I must have sounded gruffer than I realized because she startles and brings her gaze back to the present and not whatever past she was seeing out the window.

She gives me a half-hearted smile when she says, "Let's not talk about that right now. I've had a great day, and there's no need to darken my sunny, blue skies."

She's hiding something. Not only is she hiding something, but I get the feeling what little bit she said was more than I should have expected to have gotten from her. She's loosening up and I just need to be patient.

*Patience is not something you have mastered, McKinley. Good luck.*

She changes the subject by asking a million

questions about the island. Our meals arrive and they are delicious, as usual, but with the company, more wine, and eventually watching her eat her dessert, this meal has never tasted better. She has a million plans in her mind and some great ideas, but I can tell she is doing everything she can to keep me talking about work and the island so we don't venture back into personal territory

Eventually, we take our leave, and our driver takes us back to the hotel. She is quiet on the ride back, and I let her have her space and don't instigate conversation.

When we enter the lobby of the hotel, I stop by the front desk and ask for my messages. There are several, as usual. What I wouldn't give to just have one actual night off. To not be tied to my work and to live a normal life. I do live a privileged life, but there are days I would love a break from it all. At least here on the island, I am free of the random paparazzi that hound me from time to time, usually when London has done something newsworthy.

She heads to the stairs while I'm at the front desk, and I call out for her to wait for me and she does.

"No elevator?" I ask when I catch up to her.

"After that night of indulgence, I think a few flights of stairs will do me some good. Besides, it's only three floors." She notices the stack of messages in my hand and holds hers out.

"Well, let's go for a walk around the property then. Burn off some calories."

Her answer is a simple nod.

"Did you want me to take those for you? I probably should have been the one to check on those. I am so sorry, sir. I'm getting used to this new role, and it completely slipped my mind. Here let me take those off your plate for you."

"I don't expect you to handle my personal messages for me. I love that you want to dive in and get involved, but I don't expect all of that."

I guide her to the gardens, and I love the brief moment that my hand touches the small of her back. She's like a magnet, and I am completely drawn to her.

"You are a busy man. I have no idea how you do it. You never get rattled. Not even your father seems to get to you."

At just the mention of my father, I go cold, but she carries on.

"I mean, I know you've known him your entire life, but he is still quite a force to be reckoned with. If I'm being honest, he scares the bejesus out of me."

"He has that effect on a lot of people. He can be very terse."

"Is your family close?"

I see, now that the evening is ending, and we're talking about *my* family, she wants to get personal. Nice try, gorgeous.

"We're as close as we can be. You've met my father. He's not the warm and fuzzy type."

How do I explain my relationship with my father? Nobody really knows the truth about it, but she is the first person I feel like I want to tell. The first person I could trust.

Not yet, though.

We spend the next few minutes walking the property in silence, and much too quickly we're taking the stairs to her floor. Before I know it, we've reached her room. She seems reluctant as she unlocks the door, and I can't help but wonder what's going on in that beautiful head of hers.

She steps into her room but leans against the door jam and holds the door open. "Thank you for a lovely meal and for bringing me to this beautiful island. It was amazing to get to spend time here, and I thank you for giving me the opportunity to explore today."

She always seems so genuine when she speaks. I'm used to being surrounded by business and bullshit. Her sincerity always takes me off guard for a split second.

"It was my pleasure, Olivia. I'm hoping you won't mind leaving the island with me tomorrow, though? After hearing all of your ideas tonight, I would love to have you join me at the meeting tomorrow with the Historical Preservation Committee. I'd love the back-up when I meet with them about the old Prima Hotel. You game?"

"Oh, sir, that would be fantastic! Thank you so much for your confidence in me. I promise to sit back and take it all in. You won't even know I'm there."

Her appreciation makes my out–of-the-blue plot to spend more time with her seem like the best idea I've ever had.

"Well, I love your ideas and want you there to see what ideas you might have for this historic property. A fresh set of eyes will be good for everybody."

"I look forward to it, sir."

"Olivia."

"Mr. McKinley." She can't help the devilish grin that escapes her, because she knows this name thing is making me crazy. I think it may be a game to her now. Thinking she might be torturing me on purpose gets me a little hard, and I think it's time to bid her adieu.

"Good night, Olivia."

Stepping fully inside her door and slowly and seductively closing it, she purrs, "Goodnight, sir."

And now I'm hard as a fucking rock.

Looks like another night of blue balls thanks to the wicked woman in room 323.

It's not her fault, really. She doesn't have to do much of anything to have this effect on me. I've been in a state close to this since the first moment I saw her. If only it was simply her physical beauty drawing me in, then I might be able to get it out of my system. But there is something else at play here.

I'm not sure what it is yet, but it's distracting.

## CHAPTER TEN

*Olivia*

The skirt of my dress spins out around me, like a toddler in her favorite princess costume. I'm spinning in circles through my room, having my own mini crisis of joy. Seeing his reaction when I wouldn't call him by his first name was priceless. It gave me a feeling of empowerment to know I had the ability to so easily get under his skin.

After my day of exploring, our dinner in Avalon, and our walk around the gardens, I feel light and breezy. When my phone rings, I can't get it out of my purse fast enough. I don't know why *he* would be calling me when he just walked away from my door, but I can't help but hope it's him.

When I see Bryce's name on my phone, my mood instantly changes, and I realize I haven't thought about him once today.

"Hi," I say, trying to sound like I'm happy he called.

"Hi, Olivia. It's nine thirty. Time for our call."

"Good to hear from you. How was your day?"

"Good, how was yours?"

Oh, my God! Could our relationship be more ridiculous? I can't take it anymore. We have to talk about this.

"Bryce, what are we doing?"

"Um, talking on the phone."

"No, us. The two of us. What are we doing? Where are we going?"

I'm no longer dizzy, spinning around like a little girl in her princess dress. Instead, I've taken to pacing the floor of my beautiful suite while I finally do something I should have done long ago.

"I don't understand, Olivia. Is something the matter?"

*Deep breath in.*

*Deep breath out.*

*Do the right thing, not the easy thing, Oliva.*

"Bryce, it didn't faze you one bit that I moved to another state."

"We talk every day. It's like you never left."

"Exactly. If me being hundreds of miles away feels like I never left, then what are we even doing together?"

"What are you saying?"

I've given up on my pacing and plop down on the bed. I can't believe he could possibly be happy and fulfilled with our relationship.

"Bryce, you're sweet, and I enjoy spending time with you, but I think we both deserve more. We both deserve to be with someone who is going to miss them like crazy if they move to another state."

I'm met with silence on the other end of the line.

"Bryce?"

"I'm here."

"I'm not trying to hurt you, but life is passing us by. I think it's time we both follow our own paths and go on our own journeys."

I hear him exhale heavily before he agrees with

me. "You're right. My work is my obsession, and I probably don't give you the time you need. I'm sorry if I've neglected you in any way, Olivia."

"Nah, it takes two, and we've both have been pretty wrapped up in ourselves this past year. But I just think maybe we aren't meant to be."

"You're a good girl, and you're right, Olivia. I wish you lots of luck on your new journey in San Francisco."

"I hope you kick science's butt and find a way to save the world, Bryce."

"Thanks, Olivia. Have a good night."

"You too."

The line goes silent and it's done.

That's it.

I'm single.

Shouldn't I feel more than I am at this particular moment?

All I'm really feeling is that our phone calls are one less thing to check off my daily to-do list. I don't feel happy, but I feel that feeling of lightness I've had the last couple of weeks getting lighter and lighter by the minute.

Am I a heartless bitch?

Three years and I don't feel any sadness...just relief. I slip off my shoes, dress, and bra and slip on some boxers, roll the waistband down, and throw on my *Flashdance*-inspired, gray, wide-neck sweatshirt, and get ready for bed.

With my contacts out and my glasses on, I settle in and go over my work schedule for the next few months and make notes of the meetings I need to line up and calls I need to make when I get back to the office. Most of the meetings or events are related to art somehow. This must be a real passion of my employer as most of his travel has to do with art and not real estate at all.

*Okay, let's check out the Old Prima and see what new ideas these fresh eyes can come up with.*

I pull up the hotel we're going to try to save tomorrow, and just as I've settled in to begin my research, there's a knock at the door, and I freeze. Irrational fear takes over, and I can feel myself start to shake inside.

It's ten p.m. Why would somebody be knocking on my door? I grab my phone, in case I need to call for help, and creep to the door. Putting my eye up to the peephole, I audibly gasp when I see *him* standing outside my door.

I let out a sigh of relief that my worst fears haven't come to fruition. Now, if only my heartbeat would slow down. Knowing *he* is on the other side of the door at this hour when I look like this is a whole other thing to fear all together. I do a quick inventory of myself: sans make-up, my hair in a high ponytail, and I'm covered but missing a bra and wearing glasses.

*Shit!*

I leave the chain on the door and slowly pull it open, hoping he can't really see me behind the tiny piece of metal in front of my face.

"Mr. McKinley?"

He hangs his head and sighs heavily. "For the love of all that is holy, please call me by my name," he says mostly under his breath, talking to the ground. He sounds exasperated and shakes his head.

"Sir, did you need something?"

"Sir, really?"

The effort it takes me not to smile at his frustration is beyond any I have used before.

"Really."

He runs his hand through his hair and then leaves

them clasped behind his neck. "I just couldn't settle and have a bunch of ideas about tomorrow's meeting I wanted to talk out. Were you already in bed? Did I wake you?"

*This is not happening. Am I about to let him into my room, looking like this? This is so not appropriate.*

"No, I was still up. Just doing a little work before bed."

"Do you mind if I come in?"

*Yes, I mind!* "No, of course. Just one second."

I give the room a quick once over and make sure none of my delicates are in sight and throw the bed back together. I inhale deeply and exhale before removing the chain from the door and opening it. I stand as far behind the door as I can be, hiding myself even though I know the moment he crosses the threshold, there is no more hiding.

He walks past the door, and when he hears the door close, he turns around. His hair is disheveled, and he's in a simple white V-neck T-shirt and black lounge pants. He's wearing flip flops, and for some reason seeing his bare feet feels extremely intimate, and I can feel myself blushing. To see him so casual and out of character is disarming, to say the least. It's also extremely sexy.

*I am in so much trouble.*

"Sorry for the intrusion," he says, and I swear his eyes ghost up my body. When he reaches my face, I'm not sure what I see in them. Do I hope for it to be lust? Want? Passion?

*He's just here to talk about work. It's all in your head, crazy!*

"Please excuse my appearance. I wasn't expecting company."

"Olivia, you look beautiful. I like the glasses. A lot."

*Is it hot in here?*

I feel myself starting to sweat under his stare, as per usual, and I have to alleviate the irrational feelings whirring around my feeble body. My body that seems powerless against him, and he hasn't even touched me.

"So, I was just doing some research on the Old Prima. It's a beautiful building." I make my way to the couch where my computer is open to the images I was just looking at.

"I appreciate the dedication, and I'm glad you find the Prima as beautiful as I do. I really hope we can save it and restore her to her original beauty."

He spots the bottle of wine he sent to the room yesterday. "Do you mind?" he asks, gesturing to the unopened bottle.

"Go right ahead, sir. It's your wine. You paid for it, after all," I say, feeling a little feisty all of the sudden. *He* brings out a bit of a defiant, bratty side of me I've never known I had. I'm not sure what it is about him, but I do enjoy antagonizing him.

"Sassy, aren't we?" His attention is on me as he uncorks the bottle.

My response is to stick my tongue out at him, and he throws his head back and bellows out a laugh that warms my heart.

―――

*Ronan*

I pour each of us a glass of wine and meet her near the couch. She picks up her computer and places it on the table in front of the couch where she takes a seat on the far end, grabs her wine, and then holds a throw pillow tightly to her chest with her hand not holding her glass.

When she cracked open her hotel door, and I saw just the smallest view of her, I told myself to turn and run away, but I didn't, and now here I sit on the opposite end of the couch from a living wet dream.

I could see her long, slender neck and her exposed shoulder through the crack of the door, and I nearly ripped it off its hinges. When she finally welcomed me into her room, and I turned around and found those long legs in those short boxers, I was speechless.

But those glasses. They aren't subtle and they aren't nerdy. She's got those big, sexy, brown-rimmed glasses on, and her hair is up, giving her a *Hot for Teacher* look that has me grabbing a pillow as well. I know she's covering up the fact that she doesn't have a bra on—oh hell yes, I noticed. I need a pillow to cover the hard-on I am hoping to keep at least at half-mast.

I know I said I came here to talk about work, but that isn't true. The truth is I have no idea why I'm here. I just couldn't stay away, and I don't know what to do now. I know I don't want to talk about work, but she isn't giving me a choice right now.

"So, what can I do for the meeting tomorrow? Is there anything I need to have prepped for you?"

We talk about the Prima for a bit, and I find an excuse to get closer to her by having her pull up the images on her computer. While we admire the magnificent building I hope to save tomorrow, our legs and arms brush each other here and there, and I know I'm just making it harder on myself. I fill her glass with more wine and retreat back to my corner on the couch with my pillow and use it as cover once again.

I haven't forgotten her comment from earlier in the evening, and I know I'm pushing it. Hell, I might even ruin the evening, but I have to try again.

"Olivia, why was being alone preferable when you were a child?"

Miraculously, she starts talking.

"The truth?"

"Always."

"Well, let's just say I didn't grow up quite the same way you did. Things started off okay, but my dad had a gambling problem, and he ended up owing some not so savory men a lot of money. He started working for them, doing I don't even know what, to pay off his debt. When I was six, my father was shot and killed."

She looks away as if there is more to this part of the story she isn't sharing with me. Imagining this gorgeous woman living an "unsavory" life, as she put it, has my heart pounding with a fierce sense of protection.

"After we lost my dad, my mom and I floundered for a while and it was hard, but that was better than after they found us. The men that my dad owed money to decided my mom needed to continue to work off his debt. I'll leave it up to your imagination, but I assure you that what you're thinking is correct but worse than you could ever imagine."

She takes a sip of her wine, but she seems steady. Her eyes aren't meeting mine, but I know this is hard for her. I can see her reliving her childhood as she shares her story, and her strength is astounding.

"A few years later, when I was ten, my mom was working off my father's debt in the backseat of an Impala while I sat in the front seat with my headphones on, and there was a knock on the window. Standing outside of the car was a female police officer. She was nice enough, but she did pull me out of the car and had me wait with another officer as she pulled my mom and the man that had been paying her for sex—with her child in the front seat—out of the car."

She finally looks at me, and the hurt I see looking back at me is shattering me to pieces. My instinct is to hold her, but I know that I need to stay on my side of the couch. I can see the water in her eyes, but she doesn't shed a tear. Her strength is remarkable, and surprisingly she shares the rest of her story.

"When the officer told her they were going to take me away, she said, 'Good, take her. She's nothing but a pain in my ass anyway.' Those were the last words I ever heard my mom speak. She never came for me. Never looked for me or sent a letter. Nothing. That was it."

"Olivia..."

She puts me off and keeps talking, and I shut my mouth and let her stay the course. She's looking off into the distance again.

"I was put into the system and went from foster home to foster home. I was too old for anyone to really be interested in me. I was a gawky ten-year-old, not little and adorable. I was never adopted. Some of my foster parents were okay and some weren't. When I turned sixteen, I went to court to emancipate myself and was on my own from then on. I went to high school, worked multiple jobs, and got through it. I went to community college and got my associates degree, but I'm still paying off my student loans for the other two years when I went to Oregon State and got my bachelors. I worked my way through, but it was barely enough to have campus housing and food in my stomach."

This woman is more than I could ever have

imagined. I feel like I haven't accomplished a thing in my life compared to all she has done and all by herself. Her eyes are clear and confident again, and she looks at me with a small smile.

"With what you're paying me, I'll have those loans paid off in no time flat. So, thank you for that."

I nod my head in reply, not wanting to speak in case she had more to say. Not that I'm sure I can take anymore. My need to rescue her is screaming in my head, but as I look at the woman in front of me, it's clear she doesn't need anyone to rescue her. She's already rescued herself.

Her joke about what I'm paying her seems to have shaken off the cloud of memories that had taken her over for a few minutes, and her eyes widen when she says, "Oh, my goodness, I am so sorry. I don't usually share this part of my life. It must be the wine. I hope I didn't over share. I'm sure you got a lot more than you bargained for."

"Olivia, don't be sorry for a single second. I'm honored you would trust me enough to share your story." Even if I do feel like she left some important details out.

"Moving to San Francisco is probably a good thing too. I feel like I'm always looking over my shoulder. I know it's all in my head, but sometimes I think if I can just keep moving, it'll be harder for those old ghosts to haunt me."

"You should never have to live in fear, Olivia. If there is anything at all that I can do, if you have security concerns, just let me know. Don't hesitate to ask." Hell, I may just hire my own team of people to find these assholes from her past and take care of those old ghosts myself.

"Thank you, that's very kind, but there's no need

for that."

"Does your boyfriend know your story and that you fear for your safety?"

"Bryce and I don't talk a lot, especially about feelings. It doesn't matter, though. We aren't together anymore." She shrugs her shoulders, and I feel like the wind has been knocked out of me. "The distance just didn't work. I guess we weren't MTB after all."

"MTB?"

"Oh, that's right! You were never a sixth-grade girl," she giggles. "MTB stands for Meant To Be."

"I'm sorry to hear that."

That's a lie. I'm not sorry to hear it. Not one damn bit, but with everything warring in my head right now, I need to get out of here. Knowing she is single, vulnerable, and looking like she does, has me entering a danger zone, and I know if I don't leave right now, I may lose all of the trust I have somehow earned from her.

I lamely look at my watch and say, "Olivia, I can't thank you enough for trusting me with your story and for sharing a glass of wine with me, but it is getting late, and we have to be up early to head down the coast so I'm going to turn in."

I make it to the door, and I don't look back when I open it and say goodnight over my shoulder, because if I see her standing there in those damn boxers and with those glasses on, I may not leave, and she may file a sexual harassment lawsuit with Rose in HR.

I hear her confused goodnight as the door closes behind me, and I feel like such a dick. She shares her story with me, and minutes later I bail. Who does that? Who leaves someone alone after that?

I never thought I'd be the type of guy to do something like that, but I had to get out of there. And quite frankly, I need a smoke. I'll beat myself up the rest of the night for not being stronger. For not being as strong as the woman on the other side of that door.

God, what a woman she is.

# ELEVEN

*Olivia*

Today has been perfect.

After he left my room so quickly last night, I wasn't sure what to think. Had I shared too much? Had I become a charity case to him now? I was playing out every scenario in my head and had myself all spun up.

I couldn't sleep, so I went to the hotel gym and ran a few miles. Exercise has always been my escape. I can turn off the outside world and be in my own head for an hour or two every day. When I feel strong, I feel like I can do anything. I need all the strength I can muster working for *him*.

Last night running and a hot shower were what it took to clear my head and for sleep to find me. I told myself when I woke up this morning if he was awkward after my little bit of share and tell last night, that was just fine with me. It meant things would stay professional and make it easier to avoid crossing any lines.

Much to my relief, he has been his usual charming self today. I still refuse to call him by his first name, and it still gets under his skin. It feels great. Yes, it frustrates him, but it also brings a sparkle to his steely blue eyes. He hates the game I'm playing, but I think he loves it all the same. There have been a couple of times when my stubbornness has almost backfired on me. All it takes is one of his adorable little head tilts, and I'm nearly brought to my knees.

During his presentation to the Historical Preservation Committee, he was nothing but serious and professional. Watching him work is like watching a flock of birds moving in time with each other. He's passionate about the project and knows it inside and out. This means he can swerve and adjust to any roadblock thrown in front of him. He has an answer to every question and his intelligence is undeniable.

There is something about this man when he has on a suit and tie. His demeanor changes. He doesn't smile as much; his posture is tighter and his words come out formal. From the outside looking in, you would think he was your typical uptight rich guy, but once that tie comes off or it's just the two of us in his office at work, he becomes the man I find myself becoming more and more attracted to. Here in this luxurious convertible, we've been cruising the coast in all day, and he couldn't be more casual and relaxed. He couldn't be more perfect.

After the breakfast meeting that he kicked much butt at, we spent the day hitting all of his favorite spots along the coast. We stopped for lunch, and to say that seeing him with his suit jacket and tie off with his sleeves rolled up as we sat under the sun outside of his favorite taco stand wasn't sexy as hell, would be a lie. Sitting next to him all day watching his dark hair mussed from the top being down and with his sunglasses on has been like sitting next to a living breathing Calvin Klein ad.

How often do men like him come around? Smart and funny. Wealthy yet kind. Handsome and sexy as hell. He is a freaking unicorn, and how nobody has snatched him up is beyond me.

We've talked and laughed all day long. We

haven't gotten deep again, and neither of us is sharing any dark secrets, but things have still felt intimate. The only time he mentioned anything about our talk from the night before was when he asked me if I had ever tried to find my mom. If I had looked her up or knew if she was still alive. I was honest and said I did wonder what had happened to her but that I had not tried to find her.

I didn't elaborate, and I didn't tell him that if I were to find her and she rejected me again, it would hurt too much. I've worked too hard to feel as strong as I do, and I can't risk going backward. His question has been tumbling around in my mind all night, though.

He accepted my answer and dinner went back to the relaxed, carefree conversation it was before. I know he's my boss, but I can't help the closeness I feel with him. It's new and exciting. To be quite honest, I've never felt this comfortable around another person before.

What is that about?

Now we're on our way back to the hotel, and the night is coming to a close. There hasn't been much conversation since we left the restaurant, and that's okay. It doesn't feel uncomfortable, but I do get the feeling there is something on his mind. Maybe he's worried about this morning's meeting? He *is* running a company and must have a million things on his mind at all times. He's continuously answering emails and so am I, for that matter. The meeting requests and event invitations never end. I have no idea how he does it all. I learned during dinner that he's on a rugby team to top it all off.

Whatever rugby is?

We're staying in Laguna Beach tonight, and I must say, I will miss my room and perfect little balcony on the island. But, with the quiet that has filled the car since we left the restaurant and the wind singing me a lullaby, all I can think about is a hot bath and a good night's sleep.

*He* is still quiet when we get out of the car at the new hotel. He doesn't say anything on the short trip to my room on the tenth floor. He is still silent when the doors open and unexpectedly, I feel his hand on my lower back as he escorts me on to my floor.

He has been a gentleman before to be polite, but this time his hand doesn't leave my back. In fact, the closer we get to my room the thicker the air seems to grow. I feel like something is about to happen, like something has just changed but how or why, I have no idea. Something feels different, though. Including the fact that I want nothing more than for him to stay.

*Remember, Olivia...he's your boss.*

With my room in sight, I start to open my purse to find my room key, but I drop it when he suddenly but gently pushes me against the wall and kisses me madly. One of his hands is holding tight to my hip while the other is holding my cheek. On instinct, my hands are in his hair, and I feel myself pulling him closer and kissing him back.

As much as my mind has told me all day that I can't cross any lines with him, I have never wanted to be kissed by a man the way I have been dreaming to be kissed by him.

This kiss, though...this kiss is better than any dream. I can feel the passion and lust through the vibration of his moan that shoots right to my core. His lips are a warmth I have never known and don't ever want to give up. But much too soon the kiss slows, and he is giving me soft pecks that almost feel like he is worshiping me.

A man like *him* worshiping *me*?

But when he starts to speak between kisses, and I can feel the breath of each word where he leaves them on my lips, my world is flipped upside down.

"I always have seven things going at once." He places a kiss on my cheek.

"I'm always in motion." A kiss to my neck that nearly takes my knees and has me falling to the floor.

"When I'm with you, I feel settled." His lips find the other side of my neck. Thank God, he's holding on to me.

"Calm." A gentle kiss on my lips.

"Like I don't have to tackle everything at once and that there might be more to life." One last kiss to the lips and then his forehead is resting against mine.

"You do that to me. Thank you."

He releases me and bends down to pick up my purse and hands it to me. He places a soft kiss to my forehead and leaves me glued to the wall.

I can't move.

I can't speak.

I watch him walk away with his hands in his pockets until he turns and reaches the stairs, vanishing from view. He didn't look back, and he didn't say goodbye. Just a kiss to the forehead and a thank you.

What the hell was that?

I can feel my empty heart unfurling from this man's kiss.

I have never felt so much in my life. I have never been so confused in my life.

I bring my fingertips to my mouth and try to come to terms with the reality that what I'm still feeling lingering on my lips, neck, and face really just happened. I close my eyes and try to remember every moment and every word and hope the memory never fades.

In a trance, I finally find my key and stumble into my room.

———

It's Sunday morning, and my eyes slowly creep open to the sun peeking through my curtains. I stretch and in an instant, the memory of him pressing me against the wall and taking me in a kiss comes rushing back, and I couldn't be more awake, my eyes popping open, wide as saucers.

I changed my hot bath to a cold shower and stared at the ceiling for what felt like forever before falling asleep last night. It's a relief to know that there are no meetings planned for today, and it's his only day off for the foreseeable future. I'm not sure where he's staying, but I know it's not here at this hotel, and I am sure he has plans for his day. This means a day without seeing him and a day to try to clear my head.

I seem to be doing a lot of that lately. At least the trying part.

I hear my phone chime from the bedside table, and when I see *his* name and a short text that says he'll be here in thirty minutes and to dress casually, it's clear there will be no clearing my head today. What does this mean? Is this work related? Is it not?

He didn't ask me if I wanted to spend time with him on my day off, just like he didn't ask me if I wanted to kiss him last night. He told me when to be ready and how to dress. The old me, of just weeks ago, would tell him where he could stick his demands, but for some reason, it doesn't bother me like it should. Instead, it does quite the opposite. This is why I find myself jumping out of bed and nearly falling on my face when I trip over my shoe. I know better than to bounce around in an unfamiliar place without my glasses on or contacts in, but I laugh at myself and rush to get ready.

Exactly thirty minutes later, there's a knock on my door and an insanely handsome man waiting to greet me. Holding the door open to him, my stomach flips, and my heartbeat comes to life.

"Good morning, Olivia," he says, sounding more like his professional persona, even though he's standing in front of me in another white V-neck T-shirt and black shorts.

"Morning," I sing.

I'm in a great mood, and I couldn't hide it if I tried.

"How does breakfast sound?"

"Perfect."

I close the door behind me, and we start toward the elevator. Once there, we both face forward and wait in silence. When the doors open, he uses his hand to hold them ajar, and as I pass, his eyes find mine and he says, "You look beautiful."

"Thank you," is all I can say as the heat of my blush covers me from head to toe, and my stomach continues its happy little parade of somersaults.

Not another word is spoken on the drive to a little restaurant called Madison Square & Garden Cafe. It's a quaint little place where you walk up to order inside what feels more like a home decor shop than a cafe. Once you've ordered, you step out into a backyard oasis filled with fountains, sculptures, and art filling every bit of space available. The sound of the busy highway disappears, and it's as if we're in our own little world when we take a seat at a quiet table under an umbrella and sip our morning caffeine.

Other than to place his order, he still isn't

speaking. He seems angry or on edge somehow, and I can't take it anymore.

"Mr. McKinley, have I done something wrong? I know it's your only day off, and I don't want you to feel obligated to spend it with me. If that's what's wrong, please know you don't need to entertain me."

His anger seems to be building, but he still hasn't spoken. Images of last night keep flashing through my mind, and I know I need to be brave and bring up the elephant in the room...or patio as it were.

"Sir, about last night..."

---

## Ronan

"Olivia, don't start!"

She startles when I pound my fist on the table and lean in toward her. I didn't mean to react so fiercely but this *sir* and *mister* bullshit has to stop.

"I am not going to ask you again. Please, for the love of God, call me Ronan.

"But, Mr. McKinley..."

*What the fuck?*

I do my best to remember I *am* in public, and I sit back in my chair and try to show some sense of decorum, but inside I am seething.

"Are you serious right now? Are you telling me you don't feel anything?"

What she doesn't know is that from the moment I saw her standing with her tablet in her hand in the low light of that ballroom weeks ago, I practically imprinted on her. Whether she knows it or not... She. Is. Mine. I am not going to let her pride or the fact that she works for me get in the way of what might be possible for us. It's time to stop beating around the bush and just be straight with her.

"Olivia, I know what you're going to say. I know how hard you've worked to get to where you are. I know you don't want to be that cliché woman who sleeps her way to the top, and I know you just broke up with that boring little scientist you wasted three years of your life with. Well, I don't want to waste another minute not getting to know you. We can take it slow, if that's what you want. All I know is that it feels good to be near you, and it felt amazing to touch you last night. I know it breaks every rule, but I've lived my life following rules, and I think I deserve to break at least one. Time with you seems like a worthy reason to break a rule or two if you ask me."

Her mouth is still open from when I interrupted her, and her beautiful doe eyes are wide. She finally closes her mouth when the server delivers our breakfast. I've shocked her, and she seems as confused as I am. But screw it! I tried to keep it professional. Okay, I didn't try that hard, but I did bail after hearing about her break-up, and that was a herculean effort.

But fuck it! I've lived a cold, gray life, and this woman brings me color and warmth. I didn't know I was living such a miserable, dreary life until she arrived. She's the one I didn't know I was waiting for. We'll figure the rest out later.

The only sound I hear, for what seems like an eternity, is the bubbling of the water on the rock fountain next to our table, when she finally speaks.

"Mr. McKinley..."

*Is she fucking kidding me right now?*

My fork drops to my plate in a loud clank. I start

to open my mouth to scold her yet again, but she lifts her hand, asking me to let her speak. I clasp my hands in front of me and sit back in my chair.

"Mr. McKinley, what if I don't return the same feelings for you?"

My heart drops to my gut. I swear I thought we were on the same page.

"You *are* being a bit presumptuous. You're just telling me how things are going to be without even asking me what *I* want."

She's sitting back in her chair with her arms crossed in front of her. *Shit*! I know I'm not crazy. I know she feels something.

"Olivia...I mean Miss Adams..."

She cuts me off again. I guess it's still her time to speak. "How do you know if we try this, it won't be just to break the rules, to try something new and forbidden?"

Solid point, but I know there's more here. She continues...

"How do you know I'm not after your money?"

"I know you better than that," I reply without hesitation.

She lifts an eyebrow at my answer. "How do you know I don't just want you for your body?"

A slow grin, that she can no longer hide, forms on her gorgeous face, and I'm finally in on the joke. She's messing with me.

"You feel it too." It's not a question. It's a statement, and she nods her agreement.

Bravado gone, she uncrosses her arms. Looking nervous, almost sheepish, she lifts her hand to take a drink of her orange juice, and she's shaking.

When she puts the glass down, I take her trembling hand in mine. "Your pace. I don't need anything more than to be near you. Do you hear me? Your. Pace."

Our fingers tangle together, and as calm as she makes me, this simple gesture lights off every nerve ending in my body, and I swear I'm seeing colors I've never seen before.

"There's somewhere I want to take you after breakfast."

She nods and is back to seeming unsure when mere moments ago she seemed in such control.

*I know exactly how you feel, gorgeous.*

## CHAPTER TWELVE

*Olivia*

As soon as we walk out the front door of the sweet little restaurant, he takes my hand in his. The feel of his warm hand engulfing mine is enough to keep me happy all day. I would walk anywhere he wanted to go as long as he was holding my hand.

It's a bit shocking at first. He seems too sophisticated for hand holding, but I am certainly not going to complain about it. We walk along the tiny sidewalk that has cars flying by on Highway 101 on our left and small little art galleries to our right.

As we casually saunter down the road, we take our time looking at the art in the windows but not saying much. When we arrive in front of a gallery called *Eclipse*, he stops.

"This gallery is full of pieces from local artists from all over the country, trying to get their start. They showcase up-and-coming artists that may not have had that first big opening yet but are on the cusp of being discovered."

"Wow, you sure know a lot about it."

"I do," he says, walking through the front door.

"Wait, I don't think their open yet," I whisper to his back as he pulls me inside with him.

There is a stunning older woman behind the

counter who lights up when she's seen him. She leaves her desk and walks up to him with her arms open wide, and when she reaches him, she takes his face in her hands.

"Oh, my sweet boy, it's been too long!" She releases his face, and they embrace in a warm hug. It's then I catch her eye.

"And who is this lovely lady?" the woman asks, stepping back from Ronan, waiting for her introduction.

"Ava, this is my friend, Olivia. Olivia, this is Ava. She runs *Eclipse* and makes a mean enchilada," he says with affection in his voice. It's clear Ava is more than a shopkeeper, and it didn't escape me that he introduced me as his friend and not his employee.

"It's lovely to meet you, Ava." I say, taking her hand.

"Lovely to meet you, as well." She's talking to me, but she's looking at her *sweet boy*. I get the feeling she's important to him.

"So, what's new with the shop, Ava?" he asks with a big smile on his face, looking happier than I have ever seen him look.

I decide to take a walk around the small space and give them as much privacy as I can while I look at the pieces of art hanging on the gallery walls. There are paintings, prints, and photographs as well as a couple of sculptures here and there, but the way it's all set up, it flows nicely. It really is a great space.

When I've made my way back to the desk, the two of them are whispering, and when he turns his attention to me, he flashes me a smile as big as the one he gave Ava only moments ago. It sure does feel good to be on the receiving end of a smile like his.

He holds his hand out to me and I take it without

hesitation. He gives my hand a squeeze and turns to Ava. "We're gonna pop upstairs real quick."

Ava sounds shocked when she replies, "Upstairs?"

He chuckles under his breath, and with a smile in his voice, he replies. "Yes, Ava. We're going upstairs. Do I need to leave the door open?"

"You need to watch that smart mouth of yours, young man."

"Yes, ma'am," he shouts over his shoulder while he pulls me through the back of the shop, around boxes and covered works of art.

We walk through a back door, which leads us outside, and then take a sharp right to a set of stairs that lead up. We take the first set and turn to take the next and end in front of a door that Ronan opens with his key. He puts the key in the lock but seems to hesitate before he swings it open. He lets me walk in ahead of him, and I feel at home instantly. I don't know what I was expecting, but it wasn't this.

I feel him walk past me, and he makes his way toward the front of the room and pulls the curtains open. I'm in heaven as the light shines in on the small apartment of dark wood floors and crème walls. There is a small kitchen and living area that leads to a set of French doors and a balcony. Simple. No frills.

I start to make my way toward the nervous-looking man in front of me, when I notice a small bedroom to the left. The all white bedding is in disarray, and I see a familiar Tom Ford suit jacket over the back of a chair.

"Did you sleep here last night?"
"I did."

I leave the doorway of the bedroom and find the

course I was on before I was distracted and find myself in front of mister tall, dark, and handsome.

"I love it," I confess.

He shrugs. "Less is more," he says with a grin, using my words.

"Exactly."

Taking my hand again, he opens the door to the balcony where there is an overstuffed outdoor couch and two matching chairs that all face the gray stoned table which doubles as a fireplace from the looks of it.

I move to the patio railing and look down at the street below and the ocean ahead of me.

"It's perfect."

I turn back to him only to find him watching me with his hands in his pockets and his face serious. Almost solemn.

"Is everything okay?"

"I've never brought anyone here before," he confesses.

"What do you mean?"

"Ava is the only other person that knows about this place and of the gallery. Not even Evelyn knows about it."

I lean back against the rail, silently letting him know I'm waiting for him to share more of his story.

"I don't want to talk about my family right now, but we aren't close, and there are some things I want to keep to myself. I own this building under a different company name, and Ava and I handle all the business on our own. It's not much. Just the gallery and this apartment."

"Was there a special reason you picked this place?"

He runs his hands over his face a couple of times

and then through his thick, black hair. His hands are clasped behind his neck, and he lets out a heavy breath. He looks stressed, like the weight of the world is on his shoulders. I don't want to force him to share more than he wants to. I can already see what a big deal this is for him.

I turn back to my view of the ocean to give him some privacy and say, "It's okay, you don't have to say any—"

"Back when my mom was in her twenties, she was an artist. The gallery downstairs was the home of her very first showing. Growing up, the only time I would ever see my mother truly happy was when she talked about her art and her life before I was born. When I found out the gallery was for sale eight years ago, I had to have it."

He comes up behind me, and I can feel his presence, but he doesn't touch me.

"Thank you for trusting me with this," I say to the view ahead of me, still giving him his space.

"Thank you for being here," he practically whispers. I can feel the want resonate off his body, but true to his word, he is letting me dictate the pace of things.

I turn to face him, and he is mere inches away, and because it feels natural, I place my hands on his chest. I can feel the beat of his heart speed up at my touch, and my own heart feels like it's opening a bit more every minute I'm lucky enough to spend with him. My eyes go to his throat, and I see him swallow, and although he is keeping his hands to himself, I feel like he is touching every centimeter of my body.

When I finally grow brave enough to lean in for a kiss, he leans forward just a hair and reverently kisses me on the forehead.

Whoa.

Who knew the effect a forehead kiss could have on a person.

It's official.

Forehead kisses are highly underrated.

He clears his throat and says, "We should go. I don't want to give Ava heart palpitations because I have a woman in my apartment for the first time."

"For the first time, really?"

"Yes, like I said, this is a first. I've never shared Eclipse with anyone."

"Thank you."

He smiles.

I take a step back from him and hold out my right pinky finger. "I want you to know your secret is safe with me." He finally gets why I'm holding my finger out to him, and he locks his pinky with mine. "A pinky swear is a promise that cannot be broken. It means a lot to me that you trusted me enough to share your secret lair with me."

He chuckles and pulls me tightly to his chest, and we hold each other for a few seconds before he places a sweet kiss to the top of my head and leads me to the door with my hand in his. As we pass the kitchen, I see a motorcycle helmet on the kitchen counter along with a pack of cigarettes, and it shocks me. I'm not sure why, but I never pictured the sophisticated business man who travels by private plane to be a motorcycle guy. I especially didn't picture him a smoker.

He follows my gaze to see what I've spied. "Riding is my release. Nobody knows it's me with the helmet on, and I'm no longer one of California's most eligible bachelors or the heir to a billion-dollar company. I can just escape reality and be on my own when I need to be. I have a bike here and one back home in San

Francisco. The smoking...well, that's a bad habit I fall back on when I get stressed but one I hate and know I need to stop."

"Did you ride or smoke last night after you left me at the hotel?"

"Both," he says, pushing my hair behind my ear gently. "Walking away from you was not an easy task, and if there was ever a time I needed a release, it was last night."

"Is that so?"

"It is, gorgeous. Let's just say I've been riding and unfortunately smoking a lot since the night of the Evers gala."

His confession shocks me, stops me in my tracks, and kicks my libido into overdrive. What I wouldn't give to crawl into that bed of his and mess it up even more. Much to my dismay, he pulls me through the door and back down the stairs. We head back into the gallery and say goodbye to Ava. All of this, while never letting go of my hand.

We walk hand in hand back to the car, and there are only a few rare moments during the rest of the day when we aren't touching. We walk on the beach, check out every little shop in town, and we take our time simply enjoying each other's company.

Later in the afternoon, we find a bench next to the sand and watch some locals play beach volleyball while we eat our ice cream. All day we've been close, but he hasn't kissed me again. I don't know where the courage comes from, but since he's letting me set the pace, I think it's time I stepped up my game.

Once we've both finished our cones, I stand from the bench, and he watches me intently. "You ready to..." I cut him off and take a seat on his lap. I put my arm around his shoulders while my other hand gently traces the outline of his jaw.

"Ronan..."

"Finally," he says, referring to me *finally* calling him by his first name. But he isn't joking and he isn't smiling. He needed to hear me say it to know I was really in this. Realizing this now, I feel bad I held out so long. Even if it was fun.

He pulls me closer and says, "Say it again." If I didn't know he was as proud as he is, I would say he almost begged me to say his name again.

I drag my fingers through his thick ebony hair and then lift his sunglasses to the top of his head so I can look him in his always stormy sapphire eyes and say, "Ronan...kiss me. I'm not sure I can wait another second without feeling your lips on me again. Please put me out of my misery."

"With pleasure, gorgeous."

The hand that was around my waist slides up my back until it's tangled in my hair, holding my head. His other hand lightly grips my chin and tugs just enough to pull me a little closer so our lips finally collide.

Our kiss is slow and measured, and there is no denying we're both savoring the moment. When our tongues finally find each other, his is cold, and I can taste the peppermint from his ice cream. I think I've found a new favorite flavor—Ronan and peppermint ice cream. The sound of a toddler screaming next to us shakes us to our senses, and we stop the kiss, remembering we're in public. He doesn't pull away, though.

Forehead to forehead, he whispers. "Please don't stay at the hotel tonight. Come back to Eclipse with me. I just want to lie with you, to hold you. I'm not ready to stop touching you yet."

"Okay."

It's the easiest decision I've ever made. It may not be the smartest, but it's too late to stop this moving train we're on.

"Okay?"

"I'm not ready either."

---

## Ronan

The moment she says, "I'm not ready either." I pick her up, cradle her in my arms, and start walking back to the car.

She hides her face in my neck, and I can feel her giggle against my skin. Her reaction makes me feel like a God damned superhero. The next thing I feel are her lips on my neck, and I am the fucking king of the universe.

She's not kissing me in an overly sensual way, but her small kisses burn into my skin like a brand. Her lips against my skin are almost more than I can take. If she only knew that since the moment she said my name, I have been a goner and have barely had a grasp on my control.

The sound of her voice finally saying my name was music to my ears. I didn't think anything could ever sound as good as my name on her lips, but then she asked me to kiss her. Then she said she couldn't wait another second to feel my lips on hers again. But when she asked me to put her out of her misery, that was the sweetest of all, and there was never a request I had so badly wanted to fulfill. The sweet taste of cookies and cream that took over my senses and the sound of her nearly inaudible moans drowning out the ocean waves as I tasted her, took over that top slot.

Or so I thought.

Then she agreed to leave the hotel and stay at Eclipse with me. She has no idea that in a matter of seconds she has made all of my wildest dreams come true. I don't need her naked and I don't need sex, although I wouldn't say no to either of those things; I really just need her in my arms.

When we reach the car, I don't let her down right away. I can't. I need to taste her again. With her arms still tight around my neck, she reads my mind and kisses me senseless.

Where has this woman been all of my life?

How did I breathe without her?

She has already found her way deep into my soul, and I'm afraid there is no going back.

I place her on her feet and press her back against the car door.

"What am I going to do with you?"

She stretches up on her toes and places a small kiss to my lips. "You're a pretty smart guy." This time her tongue traces the outline of my upper lip. "I'm sure you'll think of something. At least I hope you do."

Where did this side of her come from?

"You sure are a sassy thing, aren't you?"

She just smiles and looks up at me through her lashes...silently sassing me.

"Gorgeous, keep it up and you'll find out exactly what I've been dreaming about doing to you for weeks now."

"Promise?"

I hold out my pinky finger, and when she links hers with mine I say, "Promise. Now, get inside before you get the chance to sass me again, and I show you right here on this car just exactly what I've been dreaming of."

She opens her mouth to sass me back, I'm sure of it, so I cover her mouth with my hand, not giving her the chance. A promise is a promise, and if I have to show her right here, in public, we will both be spending time in the back seat of a police car when they take us in for indecent exposure. I can think of a hundred ways I'd prefer to spend the rest of the evening.

I break every speed limit there is to break on the way to the hotel. I throw my keys at the valet but tell them to leave it running and that I'll be right back. When we get into the elevator, I am forever grateful that we aren't alone. I might have taken her right here, and I wouldn't have made it back to Eclipse before having her. I don't know why, but all I want is to be back at my favorite place. My safe place. With her.

Nothing else matters right now.

## CHAPTER THIRTEEN

*Olivia*

I don't know what's come over me or where this sultry sassy vixen inside of me has come from, but I can't help myself around him. Ronan has turned me into a wanton woman, and we haven't done anything more than kiss, but God do I want more.

I could tell at the hotel he was making a point of not coming too close as I packed up my things. He never took his eyes off me, so I made sure to take my time as I folded my bras and panties. If only I had lingerie, but who could have planned for this? Actually, I'm not sure he would have been able to stay in the room if I had anything more to tempt him with. He couldn't get me out of there fast enough.

As we walk up the stairs to his apartment at Eclipse, I can't help but giggle when I think back to the hotel room when I was doing one last walk through, and he grabbed my hand and pulled me out the door and said he would replace whatever I forgot but that we couldn't stay in the room another second. I think the bed was too much temptation for him.

He still seemed strung a little tightly on the short drive here, but as soon as he walks through the door and closes it behind us, he looks like all is right in his world.

He throws his keys on the table and takes me in

his arms and kisses me again and again. The passion I have felt when we simply kiss is already more than the passion I felt if I were to add up every intimate moment I spent with Bryce. I already feel for Ronan, everything I should have felt the past three years but never did.

I don't want to wait any longer, so I don't.

I tug on his hand and pull him toward his bedroom where I see the bed is made.

"How?"

"I have a service come in from time to time. Fresh sheets was the least I could do for you."

"Oh."

I know it's only maid service, but is there anything this man doesn't have at his fingertips? Sometimes I forget just how wealthy and powerful he is. He could also have any woman at his fingertips, and he wants me. He knows my past and where I come from, and he still wants little old me. Ronan McKinley wants me, Olivia Adams.

"Hey, did I lose you?"

"Nope, I'm right here."

"That's what I want to hear."

"Ronan?"

"Yes, gorgeous?"

"Make love to me."

He stills.

"Olivia, are you sure? I really meant what I said. As long as I fall asleep with you in my arms tonight, that's enough for me."

"Ronan, don't make me ask again."

I finish walking inside the bedroom, stopping next to the bed.

"There's the sass. I did promise to show you everything I'd been dreaming of doing to you if you sassed me again, didn't I?"

"You did."

"Well, a promise is a promise." And without hesitation he pulls his shirt over his head and drops it to the floor.

I knew he was in amazing shape, but his body...his body is perfection. There is only the light from the street shining through the blinds, but it's enough to see his perfectly tan skin. The light shimmers over his washboard abs and the slightest bit of dark hair across his chest. The minute I see his bare skin, instinct takes over, and I can't wait to feel him skin on skin. I instantly start to unzip my dress, but he gently grabs my hand and stops me.

"*I'm* showing *you* what I've been dreaming of, remember?"

I've lost the use of my voice and have to nod my answer.

"Good girl, now let me take it from here, gorgeous."

He pushes my hair off my shoulder, and then his lips press to my exposed skin. He continues to lightly kiss my shoulder and all the way up my neck until he reaches my ear.

"Thank you for trusting me," he whispers into my ear before I feel his breath move across my cheek, and then he kisses my lips gently. His eyes are filled with intensity and sincerity. "Thank you for trusting me with your story and for coming here tonight."

"You're welcome, Ronan. Thank you for trusting me with your secret lair," I say with a smile.

"Baby, your sass does something to me, but hearing my name on your lips will keep me hard for days."

Wanting to feel exactly how hard my name on his lips makes him, I reach down and palm his erection through his shorts. He is hard and thick, and it appears there is, in fact, more to him than I ever could have imagined.

Oh yes, that will do.

His hand covers mine, and he forces me to grip him tighter. "This is what you do to me, gorgeous. Do you know how many times you've left me in this state without even knowing it? How many times I've had to take care of myself just to be able to sleep at night?"

I shake my head to answer his question. If his touch and his kisses weren't enough, his words just may be my undoing.

"Too many to count, but that ends tonight."

He turns me around and moves all of my hair so it's falling over one shoulder, and then I feel his lips leave a trail across my upper back. Once he makes it to the other shoulder, he takes a small bite that has me looking back at him. I'm met with smoldering eyes filled with lust and want.

His finger glides down my back and finds my zipper. At a tortuously slow pace, he pulls the zipper down my back. He pulls the back of my dress open so the straps slip down my arms, and the billowy fabric lands in a puddle at my feet. His hands shadow each other down my sides, and as they reach my hips, I feel him kneel to his knees.

His lips connect with the small of my back, and his fingers slide into the sides of my panties, and he begins to pull them down my body. He continues to place kisses along my lower back and hips. As he lowers the material, he trails kisses all the way down my thighs. I can't help the small gasps that continue to escape with each time his lips connect with my body. This is by far the most sensual experience of my life. He is worshiping me, and I have never felt so desired.

"Step," he instructs, so I'll step out of my panties. Once their gone, he takes the worshiping to new heights.

"Turn around," he says as he gently uses his hands to apply pressure in the direction he wants me to turn.

He remains on his knees and with the height of my wedges when I turn he is face to face with the part of me that is pulsing with need. I feel vulnerable but in the best way possible. It's a vulnerability I never knew existed. He looks up at me from his knees, and the outside world and ghosts from the past disappear.

His lips and his tongue explore my hips and across my pelvic bone and tease where I really want his mouth to go. He knows what he's doing to me; I can see it in his eyes when he looks up at me as his hands gently grab my ass checks and then slide up my back and to my bra. He deftly unhooks the clasps and then reaches up to my shoulders and removes it from my body. The cold air and the intimacy of the moment have my nipples tightening, but the warmth of his hands cover them instantly.

"You. Are. Perfect. Olivia. Adams."

His eyes and hands are roaming every inch of my body from his spot on his knees, and I am completely bared to him. Completely vulnerable. Completely his. I have never felt as though I belonged to a man. Like being with him and in this moment, were meant to be.

He continues to stare up at me, and without losing eye contact, he drags one of his fingers down my body until he reaches the place I've been desperate for him to touch. His finger finally finds its way to my bundle of nerves, which are ready to explode at just the slightest graze. And that's all it takes.

My hand finds his shoulder in hopes to keep myself steady. He has barely touched me, and it's a miracle I'm still standing. Watching what his brief attention has done to me, he knows he has the upperhand, and I couldn't care less as his finger parts me and finds me wet and waiting.

"Fuck," is all he says when he enters me, still searing me with his stare. "Baby, I have been dying to taste you for what feels like an eternity."

"Please," I practically beg him.

He doesn't hesitate, and his mouth is devouring me before I can have another thought, let alone word. While his tongue circles my clit, he works his finger in and out of me in perfect harmony, and when he enters a second finger, I can't stop the moan that slips out. My hands find his hair, pulling him closer to me. I feel him growl against me, and he brings my leg over his shoulder for better access and at this angle, it's not going to take much longer before I climax.

"Ronan, please don't stop," I plead, pulling his hair tighter, making sure he stays exactly where he is. "Don't change a thing. Right there. Oh, my God. Yes!"

And just when I think he's worked me up as much as he ever could, he changes his pace and that's it; I fall apart. If I could breathe, I would scream his name, but my orgasm is so strong, so powerful, it's ripped all ability to breathe and to speak from me.

Once he's brought me all the way through my climax and I'm finally coming down from my high and able to breathe again, he places a wet kiss to the inside of my left thigh and then moves my leg and places my foot back on the ground. He looks at me through his lashes, and once he knows he has my attention, he slowly puts his finger in his mouth so that I can watch him meticulously suck off all of me that was on him, and then he does it with his other finger. Once his sexy little display is over, he reaches down and helps me out of my shoes, and then he finally stands up.

"Delicious." He kisses me deeply, passionately, and I swear he is claiming my soul. "Simply. Delicious."

He slips off his shoes while unbuckling his belt. "Finally," I say and he smiles.

"I knew you had been undressing me with your eyes all week. I feel so objectified, Miss Adams."

"You wish."

"I know."

"You think so?"

"I do. You've wanted me as badly as I've wanted you. I'm just the only one of the two of us able to admit it to themselves before now."

Never feeling so turned on and wanted by a man before, especially a man like him, I have no idea what overtakes me a second later, but that vixen comes out again, getting on her hands and knees and crawling across the bed. I glance over my shoulder and see him watching my body move while his mouth hangs open and his hands have stopped moving.

"You sure do think you have me all figured out, don't you?" I say coyly over my shoulder.

He shakes his head and brings his eyes from where he was staring at my back-side and all that was exposed to him to my face. "All I know, is that this is so much better than my dreams."

I crawl in his direction and kneel at the side of the bed. "Ronan, take your clothes off and get in this bed before I go crazy."

He obeys my order in a flash, and his shorts drop to the floor with a thud, but not before he pulls a condom out of his wallet and throws it on the bed. And would you look at that, he was going commando. Not sure why, but that is sexy as hell and so is the sight of him. He is finally as vulnerable as I am and so perfect. I can't help but to reach out to touch his soft flesh as he joins me on the bed and lays me back on the pillows as he crawls on top of me.

I can no longer see his perfection, but I can feel it as he rubs it against me and takes my nipple in his mouth. His hands are all over me, and I feel so good. Safe, secure...sexy. He makes me feel better than I have ever felt before. I could stay right here pinned to this bed by his body forever. But I also need more. I need to feel him inside me.

I reach for the condom and take it between my fingers, and when he notices, he takes it from me. He puts his hands behind my back and lifts us up to a sitting position, and he holds me on his lap. With one hand, he moves my hair out of my face. My legs circle his waist, and we look into each other's lustful eyes, searching for unspoken words for a moment before he finds his.

"Gorgeous, I need you to know this is not a fling for me. You get that, right?"

I nod, while I run my fingers through his hair.

"Olivia, I want this. I want us. I don't care that I'm your boss. We'll work all that out. Yes, you are the most gorgeous woman I have ever seen, but the night I first met you and took your hand in mine, there was more there than physical attraction, some kind of natural pull. There is something here. Something real. I want to explore that. Together. Are you in?"

On a whisper, I seal my fate. "I'm in."

He rips the foil packet open with his teeth, and I watch with fascination as he covers himself. He lifts my chin with his finger so our eyes meet again. "Baby, I've been in since the first moment I laid eyes on you. Hearing you say 'you're in' is like heaven on earth to me."

He lifts me and slowly slides inside me, and perfection is the only word that fits how it feels to have him inside me. He is huge and sitting on him like this, I have never felt so full, but nothing has ever felt so right. We find a perfect cadence together, slow and lazy to start. He kisses up and down my neck, and when I arch back in pleasure, he takes my nipple into his mouth while his thumb finds my clit again, and I can feel myself building again.

"You gonna come again for me, baby? I can feel you tighten around me, gorgeous. I know you're close. I'll let you come again as long as you promise to come with me when I lay you back down on this bed and take you the way I've been dreaming of. Can you do that for me, baby?"

Out of breath, I gasp out. "I can't promise you that. I've never had multiple orgasms with a man before." I scream out as I feel my impending climax surfacing. "This is my first time! Oh, my God, you feel so good, Ronan. Yes! Yes!" And just like that I come again, pulsing around him. This has to be the most intense orgasm I have ever had.

He slips out of me and lays me on the bed, and I'm still riding my high when he places his body over me and his perfection rubs on my core and sends shockwaves through my body.

He takes his time kissing me and letting the aftershocks ease before he finally slides into me again.

And once again I feel whole.

He rests on his forearms and doesn't let go of my gaze. He is intense. Serious. Passionate. He feels so good, and when I pull him down by the neck to meet my lips, he devours me, and his pace quickens. The feel of him inside me and the way his body is rubbing on mine is already bringing back the ache of another orgasm.

Watching the intensity in his eyes and the emotion behind them has the ache building even stronger, and before I know it, I feel like I can't hold back any longer.

"You ready, baby?"

"Yes," I am barely able to breathe out.

"Come with me, Olivia. Come with me!" he yells, and I do as he says, and I shatter into a million pieces with him.

Watching him lose himself with me is something I will treasure forever. It's new for me. I have never come at the same time as my partner, and to be honest, thought it was some fictional myth that didn't happen in the real world.

When he lies down beside me, all I can hear is our heavy breaths and the thundering of my heart. He entwines our fingers together and holds my hand as we both come back down to earth. After a few minutes, he heads to the bathroom to clean up.

"I'm gonna get some water. Do you need anything?" he says, backing out of the room. Even without a full erection he is still impressive, and I swear I'm already an addict.

"Nope, but I am cold without you in here with me, so hurry back."

He smiles and turns toward the kitchen, and it's the first time I have gotten the spectacular view of his ass. It is so magnificent I find myself stomping my feet in the bed like a silly teenager who just got asked to prom by her secret crush. This is something I seem to be doing often. Who knew it would take me twenty-nine years to feel this way?

I've pulled myself back together by the time he returns, and he brings me a glass of water too, because he is just that kind of guy. I take a drink when he hands it to me, almost gulping the entire glass down. I had no idea just how thirsty I was. He already knows me better than I know myself.

He gets back into bed, and I lay my head on his chest and run my fingers in circles through the light smattering of hair. The room darkens as a cloud passes in front of the moon.

"How am I going to keep my hands off you at work?" he says, with a squeeze to my butt.

"I think you'll manage just fine. Besides, you're a different person at work. It's like as soon as that suit jacket goes on, you are Mr. Professional and sometimes even a little cold. Especially, when your dad is around. So, I think you'll be able to handle yourself just fine."

"Am I that bad?"

I look up at him just as the moon fills the room once again, and his luminous eyes that capture me in their depths so easily glow in the moonlight.

"Nah, it's only when you're in meetings or dealing with your dad. Your staff all know how much you care about them, and you are never demeaning. They just don't get to see the T-shirt and shorts version of you that I see." I kiss his chest. "Besides, you're a mogul. You're supposed to be serious and bad-ass. I think it's sexy."

"Is that right?"

"Whatever, *Most Eligible Bachelor of California*. You know you're sexy."

"Is that any way to talk to your boss?"

"About that, Ronan. People at the office can't know about us. I don't say that to hurt you, but I refuse to be *that* woman. I don't want my co-workers to think I only got the job because the boss wanted to sleep with me. I've worked too hard to get to where I am. Do you understand?"

He pulls me closer to him and says, "Of course, and I will handle this in whatever way makes you feel comfortable. Like I said, it will be hard to keep it to myself, and I'm not agreeing to keep you a secret for long but for now, we'll do this your way."

"Thank you."

He kisses the top of my head.

"Sorry about my dad. He's a little rough around the edges."

"Nothing for *you* to be sorry about. He just seems so unhappy and to be honest, you lose a bit of your spark when he's around. Wanna talk about it?"

Because I'm lying on his chest I can't see his face, but I can feel him tense, and he goes quiet. I hope I haven't gone too far.

"It's okay if you don't want to talk. I didn't mean to pry."

"No, you aren't prying. I've just never really talked about it. Our family is big on appearances and the truth isn't always pretty."

"I can attest to that."

He huffs out a little laugh. "Very true."

I place another kiss over his heart, and I feel myself lift and lower as he takes a deep breath.

"Well, I guess I've shared my secret lair with you, so I might as well tell you about my dysfunctional family. I'm not really sure how to say this in a way that doesn't make me sound like an emotional teenager so...I'll just say it. My father can't stand me. He has hated me my entire life and has made it clear since I was old enough to remember that I was only born to carry on the McKinley name."

"Ronan, he doesn't..." I say lifting my head to look at him but he interrupts me.

Pushing my hair behind my ear he says, "It's okay, gorgeous. I've had a lifetime to get used to it."

"Ronan, he's just stern; he doesn't actually hate you."

"When the man has told you over and over that the only reason you were born was to carry on the family name, and he usually follows that up with the latest reason why I'm disparaging said family name and all the ways I am not worthy of it, that's his way of saying he hates you. You can see it when he looks at me. It's always been that way."

"I'm so sorry. Thank goodness you had your mother. I mean you bought Eclipse for her, you must be close?"

"You'd think, but no, not really. My father wouldn't allow it. I always looked forward to when my father would travel and my mother would stay home because then she would spend time with me, but that didn't happen often enough. When my mother did spoil me, or cuddle me like mothers should and my father noticed, she would get his wrath. She learned to find ways to show she cared that he wouldn't see, but she would always bow down to him in the end. Ava was more of a mother to me than mine ever was. And my uncle was there when I needed him."

"Ava? The Ava that works downstairs at the gallery?"

"Yep, she was my nanny. She's the one that tended my scraped knees, read me my bedtime stories, and talked to me about my day at school. When my parents sent me away to boarding school, it was Ava who wrote me letters and who I would call and check in with. My mother loved to paint and loved art, but Ava was the one who taught me everything I know about art. It should have been my mother, but my father didn't allow that either. He didn't let her paint, and he views her days as a free-spirited artist as an embarrassment. Theirs was somewhat of an arranged marriage, if you can believe it. The merging of two great families, and since my father would do anything in the name of business, he had no problem marrying a woman he didn't love and who felt nothing in return for him."

I sit up in the bed and drag the sheet around my naked body. I need to see his face. To see if he really is as okay with this as he sounds like he is.

"Ronan, I don't know what to say? I mean it is *their* loss."

"Whose loss?

"Your parents, silly. They missed out on so much by not being real parents to you. By not showing you the love that every child deserves. My parents were what they were, and yes, my mom broke my heart, but before it all went bad, I knew I was loved."

He reaches up and cups my face and rubs his thumb over my cheek. "I'm glad you had that."

"And I wish you had too." I take his hand and bring his palm to my lips. "Ronan, I am sorry, but no child should have to grow up without the love of their parents. Especially, when your parents were there in the same house. Your dad is a real asshole. I thought his persona in the office was just that, a persona, to intimidate those that worked for him, but he's a real piece of work. It breaks my heart that you didn't have the love of your parents and that they missed out on the joy that a child should bring into their lives." My hand is gliding through his hair, and I hope it is soothing him as much as it is me. "I'm glad to hear you had Ava and your uncle, but I know it's not the same as the love of your parents."

"Ava really was a godsend. I'm closer to her than anyone else in my family. My parents let her go once I went away to boarding school. After Ava was gone, I just stayed on campus and didn't come home on breaks until I was able to drive. Even though they hated me, they had to keep up appearances so, of course, I had a kick-ass car and everything a young man could ever want. I just made sure I wasn't home much and spent a lot of time with my friends. As long as I attended all of my parents' business dinners, charity galas, and whatever else they put on my calendar, they didn't care if they saw much of me when I was home."

He sits up in bed, and we both settle against the headboard, and he takes my hand in his and continues talking.

"Ava and I are actually co-owners of Eclipse. I wanted to make sure that if anything ever happened to me, she would still have the gallery. She took care of me, and I want to be sure she's taken care of too. She gets why I need to keep this private. She lived in the McKinley house, she knows the dynamic. I'm glad I've had her to share it with, but I have to admit, it feels even better to share it with you."

I crawl onto his lap and let the sheet fall to my waist. Being bold and brazen is something new and owed completely to this man who has so much, but has gone without even more his entire life.

Leaning forward, I place my lips over his heart. "It means a lot to me that you would share this part of your life with me." I take his hand in mine and interlace our fingers together while he takes his free hand and with one finger traces the curves of my breasts. "I'd say you turned out okay, if you ask me."

"Olivia?"

"Yes," I whisper as my head falls back and I enjoy the feeling of his touch on my skin. As simple as it is, feeling his hands on me isn't something I can fathom ever getting used to.

"You overwhelm me."

His words bring my head forward again, and I find his handsome face, and he's looking solemnly at me. He looks like he may be in pain.

"What?" I ask, not sure if I heard him correctly.

"You do, you overwhelm me. I know we're just getting to know each other, and I know I'm your boss but you have overwhelmed me since the first moment I saw you. First, it was your beauty and the fact that you were the most gorgeous creature I had ever seen and honestly, I was incredibly impressed with your work."

I'm not sure why but I feel the need to pull the sheet back over my body. His words have brought back the feeling of vulnerability and have me a bit emotional. I think it's because his face doesn't reflect his words. He doesn't let me hide, though. He gently pulls the sheet off me and then rolls me onto my back while he leans on his forearms and moves my hair off my face and continues with his painful declaration.

"But when you turned down my first job offer I was more than intrigued. When we met on the boat, and you called me out and told he how you thought, *less was more*, that was it. Your conviction. Your sass. You weren't intimidated by me, and you weren't just going to sit and look pretty. Your work and your credibility matter to you. You know your worth, and you aren't going to jeopardize it for anything. Not for wealth and certainly not for a man."

He kisses my speechless mouth, leaving me breathless. How can I feel so much for him this quickly? Why do I feel like I belong to him?

"If you hadn't come to work for me, I would have found another way to have you in my life. After that night on the boat, there was no going back for me. I knew I would never meet another woman like you. I knew if I was your boss, it wouldn't be the ideal scenario...but it meant I would get to see your spectacular face at least five days a week. So, like I said...you overwhelm me, gorgeous."

I take his face in my hands and make him look at me. "Then why do you look so miserable?"

"Because, you scare the shit out of me, Olivia."

"*I* scare the shit out of *you*? Have you met you? What do you have to be scared of? You deal with your father on a daily basis, and he's pretty damn scary."

"Woman, that man doesn't scare me anywhere near as much as you do. Nobody has ever scared me like you do. I'm afraid you have the ability to bring me to my knees if I'm not careful."

"I recall you dropping to your knees all on your own earlier tonight. That was all you, handsome," I say, feeling the need to bring some levity back to the conversation. As much as I love each and every syllable that has left his mouth, it's a lot to take in, and now I'm the one who's scared.

"Sass. Always with the sass," he says with one of his forehead kisses that feels like a deep breath and always calms me just when I need it to.

"Apparently, it's one of the things you like about me, sir."

"Did you just call me, sir? I've warned you about that, haven't I?"

"Yes, sir, you have."

"That's it! You asked for it!"

His fingers find my sides, and he tickles me mercilessly. I squeal and try to escape but he's on top of me and twice my size. I don't stand a chance. I can't help but scream in hopes he'll relent, but I am laughing too hard to get any words of protest out.

"Have you learned your lesson?" he yells over my screams.

I am barely able to squeak out, "Yes! Yes! I get it!"

His fingers stop their assault, and with the smile of a young boy, he says, "That was fun." He gets up from the bed and throws a blue Henley at me. "Here put this on. I want to show you something."

## CHAPTER FOURTEEN

*Ronan*

I'm in the living room on a video conference with the East Coast when my sleeping beauty finally stirs. My desk is directly across from the bedroom door, and she has no idea I can see her as she stretches and then, much to my disappointment, covers herself in my blue Henley again. The moment she enters my field of vision, I stop hearing a word being said on the screen. When I hear the others go quiet, I realize I've missed a question.

"Sorry, Sanders, can you repeat that?"

When she reaches the living room, she sees I'm in the middle of a meeting and brings her finger up to her lips telling me she'll be quiet. She tiptoes to the kitchen and, luckily, I can't see her lusciously long legs for a few moments when the kitchen island blocks my view. She comes back out with a cup of coffee and blows me a kiss and gives me a taunting little wave as she walks by and slips out to the balcony and covers up with a blanket while enjoying her morning caffeine. Nothing like having a rock hard erection while trying to conduct business.

My meeting wraps up, and once I've disconnected the call, I can't help but sit and watch her on the patio and think back to last night.

Last night, after I showed her exactly what my dreams consisted of and shared a bit too much of my pathetic childhood with her, I showed her my favorite place here at *Eclipse*. I put on my shorts and threw one of my shirts to her and brought her out to the balcony. I turned on the fire and covered us with a blanket, and we sat as close as two people could sit to one another.

After a few minutes of quiet and just being, she spoke. "I know I said it earlier today, but this place really is perfect, Ronan."

"It is."

"I mean look at your view of the moon. It's right there, like it's shining just for you. Your moon is so much better than my moon," she joked.

"I'll share my moon with you anytime, Olivia."

She turned to look at me and seemed to understand I meant much more than sharing my view with her. I would share everything I am with her, but I think I've spoken enough about my feelings tonight. I don't want to scare her away.

"You'll share your moon with me, huh? Wow, I don't think anyone has ever offered to share their moon with me." She reached up and ran her hands through my hair. "Thanks, handsome. Do you come with a lasso, so you can rope it for me too?"

"Don't sass me, woman. That's a very special moon. I've never shared it with anyone before, so you better realize how special you must be."

All humor was gone, and we just stared at each other while her hand continued to run through my hair.

"You're pretty special too." She leaned in and kissed me sweetly, and because we don't have control over what's happening between the two of us, we wordlessly lay back on the couch and quietly made love underneath the moon and the stars.

Seeing her back out on the same couch this

morning has me itching to recreate the moment.

"Good morning, gorgeous," I say, standing in front of her and taking her cup of coffee out of her hands and placing it on the table in front of her.

"Good morning, handsome," she says opening her blanket to me in an offer for me to join her on the couch. "I must really like you if I just let you take my coffee away from me like that."

"Hopefully, what I'm about to give you will wake you up even more than your coffee."

"Oh, I like that sound of that. What exactly did you have in mind?"

I spend the next thirty minutes showing her exactly what I have in mind, and as we lounge together under the morning sun, I know that nothing has ever felt so right. I don't know exactly how we're going to maneuver what exactly *this* is, and I respect her wishes to be discreet, but I am just not sure, realistically, how long that will be possible.

"I don't want to go back," I confess. "I just want to stay right here for at least a week, maybe a month. Does that work for you?"

"It sounds divine, but I think you would be missed. Me, not so much, but I think they may notice if you didn't show up for a month."

"Gorgeous, anyone who knows you, misses you the moment you leave the room."

"You're crazy, you know that?" she says, rolling her eyes while her face floods with a blush, bringing out the sweet side of her that I love just as much as her sassy, sexy side. The fact of the matter is, she truly has no idea what she does to men and just how alluring she is.

We're both naked and sharing a blanket with our feet up on the table. I grab her and pull her onto my lap and she yelps, but once I have her in place, she curls up like a child. Yes, having her on my lap, skin to skin, makes it nearly impossible to keep from getting a raging hard-on again, but that's not what this is about. With her positioned like this, I move her hair aside and speak low right into her ear.

"Miss Adams...the night I met you I may or may not have lingered around the room just so I could keep my eyes on you. In the process, I witnessed person after person go weak in the knees after a moment's conversation with you. Male and female."

I feel her sigh on my neck. "You are so stupid."

"Olivia, there wasn't a man in that room who could keep his eyes off of you—no matter how sweet and demure you were. Your beauty is not usual, and I mean that in the most complimentary way. You are exquisite. You may be accessible, in that girl next door sort of way, but you are also sexy without having a clue what you are doing to men when you simply stop and introduce yourself."

"Ronan..."

"I saw men get hard on the spot, and because you were so sweet and unassuming their wives just smiled and shook their heads. You have an effect on every person you come in contact with. Evelyn noticed it instantly. You just have that thing, baby."

"Well, I still say you're crazy, and whatever this *thing* is, I hope you know it's all yours."

"Is that so?"

She stiffens in my arms.

"What?" I ask her, wondering what I could have said to make her uncomfortable.

"I know it's only been twenty-four hours and this is all new, but I don't date around, Ronan. I know I just ended a relationship, but there wasn't really a relationship to end, and I never would have let this happen if I hadn't already ended things with him."

"Oh sweetheart, I thought I was actually pretty loquacious last night—for a guy anyway—but if I need to clarify and make sure things are crystal clear for you, I don't mind setting things straight." Sitting her up so she can see the conviction on my face. I make clear my intentions. "Olivia Adams, I am not sharing you with anyone, and I certainly hope you don't want to share me either?"

With a shake of her head and a shy smile, she says, "Nope."

"Good. Glad that's out of the way."

"What about the fact that I had sex with you the day after ending my previous relationship? Kinda slutty?" She brings her arms around her middle, and I think the speed in which we're moving may have hit her.

"Olivia, when was the last time you had sex with Bryce?"

She gasps, "We don't need to talk about that!"

"I can handle it. Tell me," I demand.

"Why are you doing this?"

She throws herself off me and pulls the blanket tightly over her naked body. I don't answer her and just wait her out. She needs to get over this because I am not worried about science-geek, Bryce. All it took was her confessing she had never had multiple orgasms with a man before, and any insecurity that could have ever been remotely possible from my side of things vanished.

Nope, I am not worried about little old Bryce.

"Fine! It's been weeks. We only saw each other once a week, if that, and if he was wrapped up in work, we didn't even do it then. It was boring and didn't make a bit of difference to me if we had sex or not. If I had it once every two weeks for the last three years that was pushing it. There, are you satisfied? Now you know all about my pathetic sex life. I'm sure you have women hanging off you wherever you go, and all you have to do is snap your fingers and you'll have some perfect ten waiting to be at your beck and call!"

She crosses her arms in a huff, and I can't help but chuckle at her dramatics, and when I do I get a smack to the chest from the fired-up beauty next to me.

"Are you finished?"

"Yes," she huffs with her arms crossed again.

"Well, now that your little hissy fit is finished..."

My comment earns me some side-eye, and I swear she looks like she wants to stick her tongue out at me but just can't bring herself to.

"If you're finished, let me set things straight. Was there a time in my life where I had a different woman most nights? Yes. In my twenties, I didn't just ride my bike to blow off steam. I used women and I partied. But I also worked my ass off. I didn't have time for relationships. I was busy working my way up through EVC and convincing my father and my uncle to create the real estate division of the company and that I was worthy of running it. I took that part of my life very seriously. Still do."

"I understand. I would never want to get in the way of that."

"I'm not finished."

"Oh."

"Some years back, I realized I had gotten where I wanted in the company, but my personal life was crap. I became an adult, bought a house, upgraded my boat, and worked really hard, but I haven't had anyone to share any of it with. I need you to know that I don't sleep around like I used to. That being said...it doesn't mean that I haven't had sex in years, but it does mean that my dating life may not be exactly what you think."

"It could be, though," she says, finally smiling, even if it is dripping in sass.

"I suppose you're right, but the women I meet in my circles all want the same things. Prestige and money. They don't want me; they want my name. There haven't been many in my life that actually know the real me."

She climbs back onto my lap. "This is where I'm supposed to say how sorry I am for your lonely life, I know, but I just can't. I know it's selfish, but we might not be sitting here under this blanket, naked in broad daylight, if it were different, so..."

"Kiss me."

"Yes, sir."

## CHAPTER FIFTEEN

*Olivia*

  Wanting the time to ourselves, we decide to drive back to San Francisco Monday afternoon instead of flying back Tuesday morning. The drive had moments of silence and moments of us both screaming at the top of our lungs while singing along to the songs coming through the car stereo speakers. We took our time, stopped and ate, and then about two hours outside of the city, we stopped at a quaint bed and breakfast and stayed the night.

  We shared a hot bath together and explored every inch of each other's bodies inside and out of the tub. We made love leisurely throughout the night and again this morning. Wanting to avoid morning traffic, we figured this would be the most reasonable way to spend our time. We've made love so many times in the last two days that my muscles are actually starting to ache, but it's more than worth it.

  I have seen so many new pieces to this man most see as an enigma, in his fine suits and his formal way of speaking while conducting business. He is sweet and at times silly. He is sexy as hell and smarter than any person I have known. Not smart like Bryce but smart in the way he looks at life. He could be a pessimist and hate the world, given the lack of love he has been shown, but I find him to be quite the opposite, and I have to say the way he looks at life kind of turns me on.

I thought this man was everything I never wanted, but he seems to be everything I could have ever dreamed of. I've never been happier, and I have also never been more terrified.

Is this really happening?

Is this all too good to be true?

When we finally leave our bubble and venture back into the city, he begs yet again for me to come back to his place, but as I have told him more than once, we need to get back to reality. Find our new normal. I am not moving in with him, so our new normal will include spending nights apart, and we need to start that tonight. Not to mention, I need a few hours on my own to get my head out of the clouds and find my footing again.

Ronan has disarmed me.

He has taken my strong, tough woman persona and flipped it on its head. I have gone from a woman who prefers to be on her own to wondering how I am going to breathe air without having him near enough to touch in just a matter of forty-eight hours. Yes, it was happening before then but until he kissed me, it wasn't a full-fledged addiction. Now...now I have a real problem.

Because I have prevailed, we are now at the St. Francis, and Ronan is giving his keys to the valet. He helps me with my bags, and we take the elevator up to my floor. The ride is quiet, and unlike in the movies, he doesn't reach his hand up my skirt or kiss me madly. Instead he holds my hand and rubs his thumb back and forth across my skin.

When we exit the elevator, he isn't in a rush, and the speed in which his long legs usually carry him is sluggish. He follows me inside and puts my bags in the bedroom of my suite. I follow him and am not the least bit surprised or apprehensive when he pulls my dress over my head and then undresses himself before meeting me in the middle of the bed.

We don't speak, and he does nothing short of worshipping me, as he always does. This time, it feels like he is trying to crawl inside of me and brand my soul so I don't forget him between now and when I see him at the office in the morning. He doesn't need to worry about that, but I am certainly not going to stop him from doing whatever he feels he needs to do, if this is the result.

"Don't make me leave," he says after we've both climaxed, and he's lying on his side, lazily tracing the curves of my body with his finger.

"I'm not *making* you do anything, but I do think it would do us both some good to have our own space. A lot has happened in the last few days, and we've moved pretty quickly. We need some distance so when we see each other at the office, we can behave with some sort of decorum. You feel me?"

"I feel you, and I know you're right. Besides, I went from working twenty-four hours a day to barely returning emails these last few days. It will do me some good to go home and catch up. Thank Christ, I finished up most of the big deals we had in the works last week. Otherwise, I would be in financial ruin all thanks to you. You are quite the distraction, Miss Adams. Work should be interesting."

"So, what you're saying is, I'm right. I believe that *is* what I hear you saying, Mr. McKinley."

He slaps me lightly on the butt and then drags himself out of bed. "It doesn't pain me at all to tell you when you're right, Olivia. I have a feeling it's going to happen often, so I might as well start saying it now."

"Well, we're off to a good start then. Now, since you've pleasured me one last time today, be on your way, stud."

"I'm not sure what part of that sentence caught my attention the most. You using me for my body and then kicking me out, or you calling me stud."

"I told you at breakfast the other day that there was a chance I was just using you for your body. You were warned," I remind him as I start to drag myself out of bed as well.

"Stay," he demands, while gently pushing my shoulder and laying me back down.

"Excuse me?"

"You. Naked in bed. Stay just like that. I want this to be the last thing I see of you before I leave. You look perfect," he says as he pulls the sheet down so one of my breasts is exposed.

Of course, this move has me biting my lip and feeling turned on yet again. It's impossible not to be in a perpetual state of arousal when he's in the vicinity, but when he says things like that and does things like this...I don't stand a chance. If his plan was to get me to change my mind and ask him to stay, it's almost working, but I know I need to stay strong on this. I need a few hours to clear my head. To make sure whatever this is between us is enough to risk my career and reputation.

As if putting on a show for me, he slowly gets dressed, all the while holding my stare. I know he wants to stay or have me go home with him, but I can tell he knows it is best for both of us if he goes home alone.

Neither of us has spoken since he demanded I stay in bed. Once he's finally dressed, he leans over me and places a kiss to my forehead.

"See you in the morning, gorgeous."

And with that, he leaves and I am left feeling blissfully happy and wishing I hadn't had the great idea for us to spend the night alone.

I miss him already.

## CHAPTER SIXTEEN

*Olivia*

It's not the big black building with fifty-four floors of business, power, and wealth I've entered that has me stressed. No, it's the fear of seeing Ronan again. Walking through the front doors of the EVC building, I keep telling myself I will be able to do this. I *will* get through the day without anyone in the office noticing that I've just spent the most intimate moments of my life with my boss.

With the sound of the ding that alerts me to the elevator that will take me up to the thirty-fourth floor, I start to sweat.

*Do they know?*

I think I'm losing my mind because I swear every person on this elevator knows I'm sleeping with my boss.

Of course, I was so consumed by Ronan that it felt like every person I passed on the street must have seen it written all over me.

I feel stronger, more confident, yet scared to death. Having hours to myself last night gave me time to think. I thought it would give me time to clear my head, but it really just cluttered my mind even more.

I had time to sit back and realize he did want me from the start, and even though he said he noticed my work at the gala, would I have been offered this job if he wasn't attracted to me? Did I earn this job? Did he change the position to be more of a personal assistant to have me closer?

Do I care?

Of course I do, but do I wish things were different?

Not if it means he and I had never happened.

I may be naive and have hearts circling my head, but he seems worth it.

*We* seem worth it.

I'm early and the office is still dark and quiet. My first instinct is to rush to his office to see him, but I digress. I go about my morning, turning on the lights, booting up my computer and going through the mail that was waiting for me. I start the coffee in the breakroom and check my voicemails. Now, I've done everything I can to stall, and it's time to bite the bullet and face him.

Why am I so nervous?

Maybe I'm afraid that in the light of day and back in the real world, he will have changed his mind and realized I was right from the start, and he shouldn't be involved with his employee. His personal assistant, no less. If that's the case, I will deal with it and walk away having had a beautiful few days with a beautiful man.

I knock on his door with his mail in hand and walk in a heartbeat later like I have since my first day. Just like Evelyn trained me to do. I gasp when I open the door to a dark room that looks like it hasn't been touched in days. My mind starts racing with worry.

Where is he?

Is he okay?

Did he change his mind and didn't want to face me?

This is so unlike him. He hasn't even left a message saying he was going to be late or to reschedule his morning meetings. I can feel myself starting to panic, but I push through and place his mail on his desk and open the blinds to let in the morning light.

"Gorgeous," says a deep voice from somewhere I can't see.

I gasp again and spin around in the direction of the husky morning voice I have already become accustom to and missed terribly this morning. I can see the door to his office bedroom is open but it's dark, and I can't see him.

"Ronan?"

"What time is it?"

"It's almost eight," I say, flipping on the light to his plush little cave hidden in the recesses of his office.

"Shit, I overslept," he says, stretching. "Sure, is nice to wake up seeing you first thing."

"What are you doing here? I thought you went home?"

He yawns and then sits up in bed and pats the space next to him.

"No way," I protest from the doorway. I don't dare set another foot closer.

"What, you afraid you and I can't sit on a bed together and not take advantage of each other?"

"Well, *I* would be fine with that scenario, but I'm not sure *you* have the self-control."

"Is that so?" He quirks an eyebrow up in that cocky way he does. "Interesting...I do recall the first time we made love, it was you dragging me into the bedroom and practically begging me to take you to bed. I'm pretty sure that's the way it went down."

He's right, I did instigate our first time together, but I would never admit that in the light of day. I ignore him and ask my question again, not sure I want to hear the answer.

"Ronan, why did you sleep here last night?"

He rubs his hands over his face and through his hair. "I went home and had planned on staying there, but my place felt big and empty. All I could think about was you, and it took everything I had not to bust down your door at the St. Francis, so I came to work. It's easier to focus when I'm actually here. Once I got here I was able to get a lot done. I stayed up half the night, but I'm all caught up." He beams at me like a proud little boy, looking for a reward for his good work.

He sees me smirking and throws the covers off his naked, Greek-god-status-worthy body and stalks toward my safe place here in the doorway.

Naked and fully erect.

"Satisfied? I'm already addicted to you and no, this is not morning wood. This is what the sight of you does to me. Every. Time. I. See. You."

He kisses my forehead and turns toward the bathroom, leaving me with a beautiful view of his backside. He looks over his shoulder and catches me.

"Checking out your boss's ass seems extremely inappropriate, Miss Adams. You better get back to work, or do I need to contact HR?" He closes the door behind him, and I hear the shower turn on.

Well, that's one way to start the day. Ronan naked is more potent than any cup of coffee could ever be. I leave him to shower and head back to my desk.

I'm not sure if it's the daydreaming about the man naked in his shower in the office next to mine or being busy on my computer, but I nearly jump out of my skin when a big vase with the most beautiful flowers lands on my desk. My breath rushes out of my body, and I feel myself blush when I realize the beautiful bouquet is filled with dark pink Catalina Island Flowers.

"Delivery for Olivia Adams," Leslie chimes, waiting for me to open the card, but I don't dare open it in front of her.

"Secret admirer?" she coos.

"I'm sure they're just from my friends back in Portland. No secret admirers for me."

She waits a few more seconds, and when she realizes I'm not going to open the card in front of her, she finally leaves. I lean over and look down the hall to make sure I really am alone before I finally gain the courage to open and read the card.

*Olivia,*

*Thank you for letting me share my moon with you.*

*R*

I hold the card tightly to my chest and am shocked at the effect his simple note has had on me. Not only did he hear me when I said this flower had become my favorite, but his simple note says so much. It's a reminder that he has never shared Eclipse with anyone before. He trusts me and that means something. To both of us.

I set the flowers on the corner of my desk and open up my inter-office instant messenger.

> **Olivia Adams**: Thank you for the flowers and for sharing your moon with me. They are both beautiful.

I send my IM and attempt to busy myself, but it's

hard when he is so close. Just on the other side of my office wall, in fact. It would be easy to thank him in the most unprofessional way I can think of, but I keep myself rooted in my chair, at my desk. Before I get to fully distract myself, I hear the ping of a new IM flashing at the bottom of my screen. The smile, which hasn't left my face since reading his note, widens before I even read his reply.

> **Ronan McKinley**: They don't compare to you, gorgeous.

> **Ronan McKinley**: I'd like you for lunch.

*This man is going to be the death of me.*

> **Ronan McKinley**: I mean, please order lunch from Tommy's for the both of us and schedule a noon meeting to go over my schedule.

*That's better.*

> **Olivia Adams**: Yes, sir. Your wish is my command.

> **Ronan McKinley**: Oh, I do love your sass, Miss Adams. You may regret offering to grant me my wishes, though. I know how you like to keep things professional here in the office. My wishes are anything but.

*I need to end this right now. Work. I am here to work. Not flirt with my boss via IM.*

**Olivia Adams**: See you at noon, Mr. McKinley.

I finally successfully busy myself and meet with Allison and Leslie to make sure I haven't left any meetings or deadlines off Ronan's schedule. These two are admin extraordinaires who work together like a well-oiled machine and have been more than welcoming.

Since Evelyn's retirement, they have taken over most of her admin duties, leaving me to help with event planning at EVC's various properties and scheduling the many art events that Ronan attends and hosts. I didn't think this would be enough to justify a full-time position, but there is a lot to schedule. Ronan is in high demand, and I learned quickly that those in high society would do anything to have him attend one of their events.

I've done more than one search of my new boss on the Internet and you would think he was a Hollywood actor and not simply a wealthy businessman. I get the need for a driver and tinted windows. The paparazzi would follow him everywhere if they could, but he and Baxter have things down to a science. As much as I hate to admit it, I get why his motorcycle would be a nice anonymous escape for him. Now, if we could get rid of those cigarettes...

I think things would have been easier on him if he hadn't been involved with the very famous London St. James when he was younger. It's hard enough knowing he comes from a very different economic background and life in general. He could have anyone he wants, including A-List actress, London St. James. Seeing the two of them together in images on the Internet was hard enough. Talking about it would make it that much more real and that isn't something I'm ready for, especially when I see her name on his schedule for tomorrow night.

My phone rings and Leslie lets me know that my Tommy's delivery has arrived. I make my way up to the lobby and am greeted by a very happy Aaron.

"Olivia, looking lovely as always."

"Thank you, Aaron. How have you been?" I say, taking the credit card slip and adding my tip before signing.

"Well, now that I've set my eyes on you, my day has improved. You still got that boyfriend?" he asks just like he did last week.

"Yes, Olivia, how is that boyfriend of yours?" Ronan says from behind me. Aaron's eyes widen for a brief second, but he doesn't seem intimidated.

"I've tried to get her to go out with me, sir, but she claims to have a boyfriend. I think it's just an excuse so she can tell me no. I'm not a quitter, though. I'm gonna keep asking until she casts this boyfriend of hers aside. If he even exists." Aaron winks.

"Is that so," Ronan says, coming closer and standing to the side of Aaron and I, placing himself right in the middle of us.

"Yep, she's worth the wait, wouldn't you say, sir."

I turn to Leslie, hoping she'll save me, but she doesn't help in the least. "I didn't even know you had a boyfriend. Do tell," she says, pretending to be put out that I haven't shared my personal life with her.

"What is wrong with the three of you? Are we not at work?"

Ronan is having too much fun with this. "We're all like family here, aren't we?" he says to Leslie.

"Sure are, sir, and family doesn't keep secrets from each other."

"Seriously? You guys are ridiculous!" I snag the bag of food from Aaron's hands and hand him his clipboard. "Sir, I'll just grab my notes and set up lunch in your office."

I flee the scene and can't get to my office fast enough. I grab my laptop and notepad and set up lunch in Ronan's office. I pull his calendar up on my screen and hear the door click shut.

"Someone seems smitten," he says, coming up behind me. He pulls my hair back to expose my neck and kisses me softly, shooting desire straight to my core.

"Ronan, stop it," I whisper, even though it's the last thing I want him to do.

"You don't mean it, gorgeous."

"I may not, but we have to give this a real chance, and for me, that means work is work. Please." I don't mean to beg, but if he doesn't stop, we'll both be naked in a matter of seconds.

Much to my relief, he walks around the table, removes his jacket, and takes a seat. "He's right, you know."

"Who's right?"

"Your admirer."

"Aaron?"

"You do look lovely today."

"Ronan..."

"And, he's right. You are worth the wait. Too bad Aaron will be waiting a very long time."

"Be quiet and eat. We need to go over your week."

"This isn't what I ordered, though."

"What?" I can't believe I messed up his order. "But you didn't request anything in particular so I ordered your usual. What did you want?"

"I said I wanted *you* for lunch, Olivia."

"You are incorrigible!" I throw a napkin at him,

and he swats it away without taking his eyes off me.

"I didn't like seeing your little ginger friend so eager for you to be single."

"He's joking. Besides, he thinks I have a boyfriend."

"I think he should know. I don't like that people have to wonder if you're taken."

"And what exactly would you like me to tell my *little ginger friend* the next time he asks?"

"I think you should tell him that you do, in fact, have a boyfriend. A boyfriend that does just fine satisfying your needs...as many times in a day as you require them to be met. Also, be sure you tell him that he's a big fellow who will have no problem kicking his skinny little ass if he lays a finger on you. I'd also prefer he stop looking you up and down the way he does, but he is just a man after all. That may not be a reasonable expectation."

*Ronan McKinley is my boyfriend?*

"Are you finished?" I ask, knowing he has to be able to hear my heart raging in my chest. I know it's all I can hear.

"I am, but I didn't see you taking any notes. Did you need me to repeat any of that for you?"

"No, I think I got it."

"Good. Now, that we've got that settled, and since you won't let me satisfy you in the other room, let's go over my calendar for the rest of the week, and I'd like an update on next month's gala."

I finally get him to focus and go over his schedule. We make a list of things he needs me to do for him, and the more we add to the list, the more I realize what a business mogul he truly is. It really does mean something that he didn't work much the last couple of days to spend time with me. The realization fills me with a warmth I'm not accustomed to but have been feeling a lot these last couple of days. As always, it feels good. *He makes me feel good.*

We go over the gala that Evelyn had been planning for the better part of a year and that I've taken over from her. It's a big event, and I'm nervous but more excited than anything else. Just as we're wrapping up, the door to his office flies open and in storms Daniel McKinley.

"So, you're finally back in the office and here you are playing footsie with your assistant! Was this always your plan? Convince me to expand the company and put you in charge of your own division so you could gallivant around with your hot new piece of ass, who you're disguising as your PA?"

Ronan bursts out of his chair, sending it flying across the room. "I will not have you speaking about Olivia or any of my employees that way. I've been away on business, and I do believe I've earned a couple of days off should I decide to take them."

I quickly start packing up my things and picking up lunch. My biggest fear is coming to life and from the last person on earth I would want it to come from.

"So, you're telling me you replaced Evelyn with a girl who looks like this and you aren't fucking her? Nice try, my boy."

"Enough!" Ronan yells. "This is unacceptable and I insist you apologize to Olivia now," he yells once more, rounding the table and standing toe to toe with his father. He has a good six inches on the elder McKinley, but he doesn't intimidate him in the least.

"Boy, you don't get to tell me what to do, and if you think I am going to apologize to a lowly assistant in heels, you are sorely mistaken!"

"Get out!" he howls.

"Again, you don't get to tell me what to do." Daniel seems calm as can be. Not budging.

I make my way to the door, and when I look back, I can see the mortification and worry in Ronan's eyes. He's ashamed of his father and worried that everything I didn't want to happen is happening, and I'm going to end things. I do my best to give him a smile of assurance and escape to my office.

Allison comes in and shuts the door behind her. "You okay?"

"I really don't know. What is wrong with that man?"

"I know it's hard to do, but ignore him. He does this every time a new woman is hired to work for Ronan and under the age of forty. He did the same thing to me when I first started. It's not okay, and I am not saying any of us should have to deal with it, but please know that none of us think the things he said."

"You don't?"

"No, Evelyn told us from the beginning how qualified you were. We know you're here because you were the best fit for the job."

I sag in my chair. "Oh, thank goodness."

What a relicf.

"Listen, he usually only comes into the office once a week, and we all just try to stay out of his way. If you hadn't noticed, *our* Mr. McKinley isn't anything like his father. Thank God."

"I know he's not, but his father is an asshole."

"Ha ha, you've got that right. Now, if you're okay, I'm gonna get out of here so he doesn't see your door shut and think he's gotten the best of you. Hang in there."

"Thanks, Allison."

She winks and opens my door and scurries back to her cubicle.

The flowers on the corner of my desk catch my eye. It reminds me that he shared more than his moon with me. He told me about his parents, and I knew he was telling the truth, but this is the proof I wish I had never seen.

Fifteen minutes later, Daniel silently leaves and as soon as he does, I hear the ping of my instant messenger.

**Ronan McKinley**: I am very sorry for my father's behavior. I am sure you want me to stay as far away from you as possible right now, but please let me take you to dinner so we can talk.

**Olivia Adams**: It's okay. I'm not upset. Allison said he's done this before and it isn't anything new.

**Ronan McKinley**: I would still like to make it up to you. Please let me take you to dinner tonight.

**Olivia Adams**: Thank you for the offer, but I have an appointment to look at an apartment tonight.

**Ronan McKinley**: I can go with you and then take you to dinner.

**Olivia Adams**: I need to do this on my own.

**Ronan McKinley**: Why?

**Olivia Adams**: Because...

**Ronan McKinley**: That's not an answer, and I wish you would let me help you, but I get it. Will you at least let Baxter drive you?

**Olivia Adams**: Not necessary, but thank you.

**Ronan McKinley**: Please.

**Olivia Adams**: Sir, you have a conference call with New York in two minutes.

**Ronan McKinley**: If I'm still on my call when you leave for the day, please call me tonight and let me know how the apartment hunting goes. Good luck.

**Olivia Adams**: Thank you.

**Ronan McKinley**: xoxo

Did the tall, dark, and handsome real estate mogul in the office next door just leave me Xs and Os?

---

I can't believe I'm lying here, lounging in *my* bed. In *my* apartment.

Okay, so it came fully furnished, and all I had to do was pack up my hotel room and wheel my suitcases over to my new building, but I signed the lease today and for now...it's all mine. It's small but clean. The kitchen has granite countertops and high-end appliances. Except for some of the art on the walls, there isn't anything I would change.

I found the apartment last night and moved in at lunch today. I haven't seen Ronan for over twenty-four hours and I miss him. It was nice to have him out of the office, though. I always work hard but he is quite the distraction.

I've been replaying yesterday afternoon in my head over and over again. I snuck into his office as quietly as possible during his conference call to leave him with some papers that needed his signature and thought I would escape unscathed, but that was not the case.

"Hey, gorgeous."

I brought my finger up to my lips to remind him he was on a call, but it didn't faze him as he rose from his chair like an Adonis.

"I'm on mute, Olivia."

"Oh." Is all I got out before he pushed me against his office door, effectively shutting it. His hands roamed my body and he kissed me fiercely. Like he hadn't kissed me in years when it was just the night before at the hotel. All the while a man droned on about ROIs and other acronyms.

"Ronan," I said, stopping his hand as it went under the hem of my dress and started to make its way up my thigh. "Stop."

He rested his forehead on mine—God, I love it when he does that. "I know you're right. I'll miss you tonight. Good luck apartment hunting," he said, kissing my forehead where his had been. Just the way I love.

That small, stolen moment got me through last night and today while he was in L.A. for meetings. We spoke on the phone, but I miss his touch.

*Gah! You are such a girl, Olivia! Get a grip!*

If I can't keep it together after one day apart, what am I going to do when he leaves for New York next week?

Today, with him out of the office, I was able to get things done and leave early so I could do some grocery shopping and move into my new home. But before the day ended, I had the pleasure of speaking with London St. James, herself. She was snotty, but I took her message asking if Ronan would be at her event this evening and added it to the email recap I sent to Ronan at the end of my day.

It's nine thirty p.m. and I'm surprised I haven't heard from him tonight, but I will not be the needy girlfriend who texts her boyfriend all day. Especially, knowing he's with London. His ex. Heck, I'm still adjusting to the fact that he's my boyfriend. I pull my throw over my legs and settle on my bed when I hear a knock coming from my living room.

Unexpected knocks on my door always have me on edge. And I instantly think I've been found. It's unhealthy, I know, but the fear is always lying just beneath the surface. Leery, I tiptoe to the front door and check the peephole and see my favorite shade of blue staring back at me.

"Let me in, gorgeous," he pleads through the door.

I don't hesitate opening the door to him, and he doesn't hesitate rushing me and taking me in his arms after kicking the door shut with his foot. He holds me tight and smells the top of my head. "I missed you today."

"That's good to hear."

Stepping back a few inches, he takes my face in his hands and tenderly kisses my lips. Gentle peck after gentle peck. His lips feel wonderful on mine and fill the void that was sitting empty all day.

"Hmmm...I missed you too."

"Good to hear," he says with a smile. "Now, show me your new digs."

My new digs are small but feel teeny tiny with him standing in my living space. He is quite a presence, and I wonder if I'll ever get used to it.

I show him my humble abode. Living room, kitchen, bathroom, and bedroom.

Swinging my arms open and spinning in a small circle, I declare, "That's it, home sweet home."

"You love it?"

"I do. It's perfect for me. I think it's cute and best of all, it's simple and in my price range. I don't have a household staff, like some people."

"I can arrange that, if you like?"

"Absolutely not! Don't you dare."

"I wouldn't dream of it." He kisses my forehead and notices the TV is paused. "Was I interrupting something good? Whatever it was I really like your outfit, you little thief."

I wondered how long it would take before he noticed I was wearing his blue Henley from the other day and a pair of boxers.

"Only one of my all-time favorite rom-coms. Care to join me?"

"That is the best offer I've had all day. Yes, please."

He slips off his shoes and removes his suit jacket and tosses it over the chair in the corner of the room. I find my spot back in the middle of the bed, and he lies with his head on my stomach and wraps his arms around me. I hit play and settle in.

Not long into the movie, he says, "I get it now. There are two clear reasons you like this movie so much. Tom Hardy and Chris Pine, right?"

"Nope, just one."

"Do tell?"

"It's all about Tom Hardy," I whisper as I run my fingers through his hair.

"Oh really, you have a thing for Mr. Hardy, do you?"

"Well, I did until I met this guy a few weeks back."

"A guy? Really? What's he like?"

With my fingers still in his hair, I describe him. "He's tall, dark, and handsome. A shrewd business man with a kind heart. Most importantly, he likes my sass."

He squeezes me tighter. "That he does."

He goes quiet, and after twenty minutes or so, I can sense that something is wrong. He isn't himself.

"Hey, handsome. What's got you so quiet tonight?"

"Just tired," he says, deflecting.

"Ronan, you don't have to tell me, but I'm here if you need to talk."

Still lying with his head resting on my stomach, he sighs deeply. "So, you know I was with London St. James tonight, right?"

Not the words I wanted to hear. I really hope he didn't just hear my heart fall to my stomach where his head lies.

"I do," I confirm.

"Well, London is an ex of sorts."

"Of sorts?"

"We grew up together. Our parents are friends, and her father is a very wealthy businessman just like mine. We spent our summers together, and our parents liked to talk about how when we grew up we would get married and bring our two great families together. Our children would carry on the St. James and McKinley empires, and it would all be a fairy-tale dream come true."

"Oh."

"I always thought that our parents were joking, like parents do, and never paid it much mind. Then the summer before my senior year of high school, we actually took things past friendship. Well, *she* took things further, and I was a teenage boy with a hot chick making moves on him and I went along. I hate to admit this, but London was my first. I never really liked her. We weren't MTB. I hear that's what the sixth-grade girls would say anyway, but we were forced to spend time together, and it made us friends by default, I guess? Later, when I was twenty or so, I tried again, for the family, but I still couldn't stand her. This was after her first big movie, and after a year of red carpets, I couldn't keep up the facade and that was that."

"You lost your virginity to London St. James? Queen of the tabloids, London St. James."

His chuckle vibrates on my hip bone. "Yes, Olivia. I did. I hope that's not the only part of the story you heard?"

"I'm sorry, she's just a tough one to compete with," I confess. But I didn't miss his reference to me explaining what MTB was the night I told him that Bryce and I weren't *meant to be* and had broken up.

"There is no comparison. I wouldn't trade you for a hundred Londons, trust me," he says, giving me a squeeze with his arm that is wrapped around my waist. "I always knew what a bitch she could be, but I had no clue until things didn't work out. The more time I spent with her the more the real her came out, and she is a vile bitch. I don't mean that to sound sexist, it's just the truth. She doesn't care about anyone but herself and doesn't care who she takes down on her way up. Anyway, she knew there wasn't anything real between us, but she didn't care. She wanted the money and the name, and let's face it...the fact that I didn't want her, pissed her off. London always gets what she wants and that was me. When things didn't work, our parents were livid and of course it was all my fault."

"Why was it your fault?"

"It wasn't, but London did what she always did and went crying to daddy about me breaking her heart. My father was livid and said I had ruined everything they had planned for the future of the company. It turns out they were serious about the two of us marrying and merging the two companies together. She couldn't stand me either, but that's not what she told our families. Now, she's a big movie star, and my father has even more reason to hate me. I swear she and my father still think it's going to happen one day. She doesn't really want me, she just continues to be pissed I broke up with her all those years ago. Her ego is still bruised fourteen years later."

"So, you're supposed to marry her?"

I can feel the fear cutting off my breath and the need to flee is raging through my brain.

Ronan sits up, putting himself in front of me, and holds my hands. He searches for my eyes, which are currently looking down at his strong hands holding mine.

"Hey, hey, baby, no. I am not promised to anybody. There is no legal agreement, and I am a grown man who isn't going to marry anyone I don't want to.

There is however, one evil woman out there who thinks the wishful thinking of our parents would really come to fruition, and now she wants her revenge. She always has. Like I said, I tried to date her, and there simply wasn't anything there, and it was never going to work."

He releases one of my hands so he can cup my face and softly brush his thumb over my cheek.

"Tonight, was a reminder of how happy I am that I met you, but also that I hate hiding you. I want the world to know I'm taken. That you are mine."

"I'm yours?" I question but can feel the small smile that sneaks onto my face.

"Without a doubt," he says quietly, leaning forward and gifting me a small kiss. "I've found you, and I'm not letting go. I'm not sure how long I'm willing to keep you a secret, but if that's what you need for now, so be it."

He ends his statement with a kiss that turns into the softest, sweetest love making we've ever had. I can't help but think this is his way of telling me he's mine, and I'm his without words.

London St. James is all but forgotten.

## CHAPTER SEVENTEEN

*Olivia*

"Gorgeous, thank you for one of the best days on record. I wish we could come down here every weekend."

"You don't stay at Eclipse often?"

"Not like I should. It is my favorite place to be, but with work and all of my travel, it's hard to get away. Besides, I've never had anyone to share it with."

"I think it may very well become one of my favorite places to be too. I hope you don't mind?" I say, not even remotely joking.

His quaint, one-bedroom apartment above an old art gallery is without a doubt my new favorite place. The smell of salt in the air and the calm of the sun and the surf alone seem to be what I was always missing. Time at Eclipse also means alone time with my favorite real estate mogul. Time is a precious commodity for someone like Ronan, and I appreciate it more than he knows.

"My moon is your moon, baby."

Damn this man and his moon. I don't stand a chance against their power.

"Thanks for sharing, handsome."

He stops in the middle of the sidewalk and takes the hand he wasn't already holding in his and doesn't make a sound. Our soundtrack is the crash of ocean waves and the cries of the birds flying above the beach. He stares at me while our fellow pedestrians do their best to make their way around us on the way to their cars in the parking lot just a few feet away.

I'm sure it has barely been a minute, but after what feels like much longer, he pulls me into his body and holds me so tight you would think he was headed off to war or something. My big tough alpha male, who never seems short on words or afraid to tell me exactly how he feels, is at a loss. I totally get it. Things *are* moving fast, but this *thing* is something you can't really put into words or control.

It's powerful.

Special.

Pulling back, I push up on my toes and kiss him lightly. "Thank you."

I kiss him again. Still gentle but with all the sincerity I want to convey when I say again, "For everything."

I kiss him again and take a deep breath. "Ronan, today was perfect for me too. These past three weeks have been amazing, and I don't want any of it to end." I steel myself for what I have to say next. "That being said, I think I'm going to start looking for another job."

All color in his face vanishes, and his expression is one of shock, disbelief, and most of all fear.

"What?"

"Ronan, I just think—"

"No," he says, cutting me off and pacing the sidewalk.

I can feel the panic radiate off him.

"It's not an option. Not yet. I'm going to figure this out, Olivia." His feet stop their steady back and forth, and he plants himself in front of me and takes my face in his hands. "You're not leaving, baby. Give me time. I think I have a plan, but it's not ready yet, but please don't speak of leaving again. Promise me."

I never meant to end our perfect day by causing him such anxiety. What I meant to do was show him I would rather leave my job than risk doing anything to damage our relationship. Hearing he is working on a plan helps, and I would do anything to erase the fear and anger seething from him right now.

"Hey, it was just a thought. I promise I won't talk about leaving until you tell me about your plan," I say, lifting my pinky finger to him.

He lifts an eyebrow as if questioning my sincerity.

"Pinky swear," I whisper, and he wraps his finger around mine.

"You know, I hear this is a binding agreement. You can't break a pinky swear, you know that, right?"

I smile up at the big, beautiful man who just proved he's not so big and tough after all. My mere suggestion at not working with him any longer got him more upset than I anticipated. As bad as I feel for worrying him, it was nice to see how much having me around meant to him.

I've spent much of the past few weeks scared out of my mind. What we have is different, and I feel more vulnerable than ever before. More afraid than ever before. It was nice to see I'm not alone, and he can feel that way at times too. His reaction may have brought out the alpha in him, but hearing him tell me it wasn't an option, and that I was never to speak of it again was kind of hot. Again, the old me, of just a few weeks ago, would have scoffed at a man talking to a woman like that. It's amazing what a man willing to share his moon will do to even the strongest of feminist.

Joined only by our pinkies, we swing our hands back and forth. Then out comes the side of me that I only show to him. "I can think of another way I can show you that I mean it. Interested?"

Letting our fingers lose their connection, he grabs my hand and turns us both in the direction of the car. His long legs are moving so quickly I'm barely able to keep up in my heels. I think he's excited to get me home so I can show how much I mean my promise. Thank goodness, the car is mere feet away.

I approach the passenger door and am caught off guard when he spins me around and pins my back against the cool window. Before I can say a word, his mouth crashes into mine. His breathing is erratic, and his hands move over me in a frantic mess as though he can't get his fill and doesn't want to miss an inch of me.

He breaks our connection and opens the back door. "Get in," he demands.

Not giving his command a second thought, I walk past him and slip into the back seat, sliding over to leave room for him, because I would sure be disappointed if I was getting back here all by my lonesome. He follows me in and shuts the door.

Not sure what his plans are, I sit patiently for all of two seconds before his hand, ever so slowly, finds its way under my dress. As his deft fingertips put on a show of caressing my sizzling skin, he gently nudges my legs apart and finds the lace he's been searching for. He teases me through the lace and kisses my shoulder. His kisses find a path to my ear where his hot panting easily pulls a moan from my throat and causes me to squirm in my seat.

The hand seducing me pulls away to lift my leg

over his and my other leg instinctually falls open to offer him all the access he desires. When he finally breaches the suddenly constrictive lace, he finds me wet and wanting.

"Fuck, Olivia."

"Ronan..."

As good as this feels, I want more. I know we're in public, but the car has tinted windows, and at the moment, I couldn't care less who might see us as they pass by.

"More, please," I beg him with my eyes closed, head thrown back against the seat. The moment I make my request, he does the opposite and removes his hand.

"Come here, gorgeous," he demands with a bit more softness, but he's still deadly serious.

He tugs on my other leg and pulls it over his lap and grabs my waist to help get me where he wants me faster. As soon as he has me where he wants me, both of his hands are under my dress, and the sound of beautiful black lace ripping fills the car. I gasp and he smiles like the Cheshire cat.

At a languid pace, he pulls them from my body and then brings them up to his nose and takes a deep, seductive breath. After getting his fix, he puts them in his suit jacket pocket. "I'll buy you all the lace you want, baby, but those were in the way. I've never needed somebody like I need you, and right now I need to be inside you."

His confession has me unbuckling his belt and unzipping his pants with an urgency that feels manic. I need him inside of me as much as he claims to want to be inside of me. The moment my fingers touch the softest part of him, I can feel myself swell, and I know without a doubt I am more than ready for him. I drag my thumb over the tip of him and wipe away a drop of pre-cum as I do. I bring my thumb to my mouth and suck the droplet away, and this move sends him into overdrive.

"God, dammit woman. Are you trying to kill me?" he asks, taking my face in hands and kissing me senseless. "Now," he growls into my mouth. He takes himself in hand and encourages me to lift myself over him, and just as I'm about to lower myself, his eyes of ocean blue reach another part of my soul when he says, "Show me you meant it, gorgeous."

I show him the only way I know how right now. I lower myself onto him until I am fully seated in his lap, and once I've adjusted to him, I start moving up and down. I've never felt so full, in so many different ways. Yes, physically, but my heart is full and the knowledge that I have this effect on a man as beautiful as he is, is one I'm having a hard time grasping, but it also turns me on in the worst way.

The friction of my most sensitive area rubbing on him as I move has my arousal growing and growing with each movement. It's an arousal so intense I'm finding it to be overwhelming and unstoppable. I brace my hands above me on the roof of the car as I contract around him and yell his name. All the while his hands stay on my ass to help guide my rhythm.

"Oh, baby, already? I hope you have more in you because I'm just getting started."

He traces the top of my strapless dress and pulls it down so my breast is exposed, but he's looking right at me. He's still looking at me when he takes my nipple in his mouth and bites it gently but follows it with a tender kiss.

Looking down on him, my hands are still above me, and I'm slowly moving back and forth on him as I come down from my high. To see his lips release my nipple and his tongue dart out to circle it has the weakness I was feeling in my legs fight for life. I fall forward and rest my forehead on his shoulder and run a hand through his hair.

His hands roam down my backside, but when his finger trails my crease and touches my most forbidden place I freeze for only the briefest of moments. My fear vanishes in an instant because I trust him.

He doesn't enter but he does lightly caress the area. With his other thumb rubbing over my clit and adding to the fullness of him inside of me, it's almost too much to take.

"Feels good doesn't it, baby?"

My answer is a rugged gasp as I try to find myself enough to reply to his question.

"Keep moving, baby, I'm close. Just keep doing exactly what you're doing. That's it baby."

"Ronan, I'm...I'm...oh shit...I'm gonna come again." My voice raises, and as all the blood in my body rushes to one central spot, I scream. "Now! I'm coming now!"

"Fuck, baby. Yes, that's it! I can feel you throbbing on me. That's it, baby. You're gonna make me come. Fuck. Yes. Yes. I'm coming with you, Olivia. Don't you dare stop!"

On the sounds of moans and screams, we come together, and my body sags against his. His heavy breathing lifts me up and down, and I can feel his heartbeat against my chest.

"I know that wasn't too classy, but I can't apologize for what we just did. I needed you. For a moment back there, I thought you were leaving and I wouldn't see you each and every day. You scared the shit out of me, gorgeous. I needed this. Thank you."

"No need to thank me. I rather enjoyed myself. Twice actually."

He lifts me up and off his lap and puts himself back together.

"Stay right there," he says, jumping out of the car. Opening the passenger side door, he grabs something out of the glovebox and opens the back door again.

"Hi, baby," he purrs, sliding over to me. "Open up for me." He puts his hand between my legs, and I open up just as requested. He starts to clean me up, and for some reason I feel insecure.

"You don't have to do that, I can take care of it," I whisper, putting my hand on his wrist to stop him.

"Shhh...I like to take care of you, Olivia."

Not sure what to say to that, I just say, "Okay." Like an idiot.

He completes his task, and I pull my legs back together, still feeling the heat and pulsing in my core. He doesn't take his eyes off of me. He's staring right at me, but I can't for the life of me tell what's going through his mind.

"You're staying at my place tonight."

An order, not a question.

"Ronan, we talked about this. It's not a good idea during the week. We'll slip up and say something about the night before and someone will notice."

"Olivia, I'm not leaving you tonight and that's that. It's not up for discussion. Hiding you is hard enough, but your school night rule is over," he says, referring to my rule of not sleeping over at his place on work nights. When I set this rule in place, it was simply because I was scared we were moving too fast, and for some reason I thought this would do the trick. Slow us down.

"Ronan..."

"Again, it's not up for discussion. This week is packed and next week is the gala. I'm not going to see enough of you. *You* are coming home with *me*, Olivia Adams."

Taking my hand, he opens the door and helps me out of the back seat and places me in the front and shuts the door. I should be embarrassed to be seen getting out of the backseat and into the front while he runs over to the curb and tosses the tissue in the bin. It's like telling the whole world, *HEY, WE JUST HAD SEX BACK HERE!* But, I don't even care. I seem to toss all common sense right out the window when it comes to our relationship.

He joins me in his luxury SUV, but he's the real luxury. He may have luxurious homes, cars, boats, and art, but the most luxurious thing about Ronan McKinley is the man himself. He is the greatest luxury I have ever enjoyed. Every moment spent with him is a gift, and if I'm honest with myself I don't want a night to go by that doesn't have me falling asleep in his arms.

He's right. With his meetings, upcoming travel, and all my time focused on prepping for the charity gala, there isn't going to be a lot of alone time. I think I may have to suspend my no sleepovers on school nights rule. Indefinitely.

It was a stupid rule anyway.

---

*Ronan*

"Oh my, God! Ronan! What happened to you?"

*Well, I guess this means the black eye and the knot on my cheek are noticeable.*

Not seeming to care that my office door is open and anyone could walk in and see the way she's holding my face in her tiny hands and the look of concern her furrowed brow gives away, she fusses over my bumps and bruises. Professionalism be damned and I love it.

"Gorgeous, it's all a part of rugby. I explained it to you. I let you know there was a possibility I could get some scratches here and there and—"

"Scratches! You call this a scratch! Ronan, you look like you've been beat with a baseball bat!" she hisses as she tries to keep her voice down but yells at me at the same time.

"It's a black eye and a swollen cheek. It will be back to normal before you know it. I guess you'll just have to kiss it all better after work tonight," I say, pulling her by the hips so she rubs up against the erection her care and attention has created.

*God damn she smells good.*

Thank Christ she pulls away when she does and has more restraint than I do because two seconds later Satan himself, my father, enters my office. My erection vanishes, and as per usual, my gut is filled with an inner turmoil that has exhausted me for most of my life.

Olivia grabs her papers off my desk, and she can't leave the room fast enough. My only hope is that she makes it to her office before my father, the bane of my existence, makes any snide comments in her direction.

"What the hell happened to your face, boy?" Fortunately, my face distracts him but not enough to stop his vulgar eyes from taking in her ass in that tight pencil skirt of hers. She clicks the door shut behind her, and I can feel my body sag in relief that she escaped unscathed.

"To what do I owe the pleasure, father?"

"Don't ignore me, boy. I asked you a question?" His voice is raised, and I'm sure Olivia and the others can hear him. I may be a thirty-four-year-old man but being chastised by your father is still embarrassing, even if they all know what an asshole he is.

"Rugby."

"You're still playing that asinine game? Guess that face of yours deserves it then. Grown men playing intramural sports. It's rather pathetic, don't you think? I guess we were too soft on you as a child and didn't teach you what hard work truly is."

"Father, did you come here for a reason or just to talk about my extracurricular activities?"

"I came here to make sure you have the confidence in that new brunette bimbo of yours. Thursday night's gala is important to EVC. and I will not let you and your little tramp tarnish our good name. Now, tell me, is everything ready? Does she actually know what she's doing?"

"First off, I am not going to tell you again...you do not get to come in here and disparage Olivia or any of my employees, for that matter! Do you hear me old man?"

"Excuse me, what did you just say to me?"

Ignoring him I continue. "Second, Olivia is more than prepared and capable. The night will go off without a hitch. Don't you worry about that. And third...why do you have to come to my office to ask these questions? Do you get some sick joy, coming down to our floor and ruining the mood of each and every person you cross paths with? Do you get off on it or something?"

My piece of shit father pumps up his chest and steps closer. He is seething and I am reeling from the surge of adrenaline ripping through my veins from fighting back.

*Damn, that felt good.*

"You ungrateful, good for nothing..."

Just as my father is about to really get going, the door flies open and my uncle rushes toward us when he sees he's walking into a heated debate that must look like we are about to come to blows.

"Gentlemen, this is a place of business. A family business, no less." He pushes on both of our chests, and we put some distance between ourselves. "Why don't we all take a breath and walk away."

"Listen, brother. This doesn't concern you. This is between me and my son. We don't need your assistance."

"Oh, but I think you do. You have a meeting on the forty-first floor in five minutes, and currently all of Ronan's staff are huddled in fear, worried their boss is going to come to blows with his elderly father. We don't want them thinking Ronan is into elder abuse now do we?"

I know Patrick is trying to calm things down, but his humor is falling on deaf ears. I hate the man standing in front of me. He may be my father, but he is a bastard, and I hate that I have fulfilled his bullshit prophecy of having a son to carry on the family business after he's gone. I'm embarrassed to share his name most days.

Stepping away from me and straightening his jacket, Daniel McKinley points at me and threatens me. "Push me one more time, boy. One more time."

*Or what?*

He doesn't realize that disowning me would be like a genie in a bottle, granting me a wish.

He leaves the room, and Patrick shuts the door and shakes his head. "I don't even want to know what the hell that was about."

I fall into my chair. "Same shit, different day, uncle."

"Ronan, you can't let that unhappy old man get to you. You're just giving him what he wants."

"He cannot come in here and disparage my staff. I won't allow it."

"You're a good man, Ronan. I'm sorry you have to put up with my stupid older brother. He's been like this all of his life, and I don't think we're gonna be able to change him now. I know you never wanted to work here, and you only do it for the family. I hope you know that I appreciate all you have sacrificed, but you don't want to spend your life miserable. There is no law that says you have to work here or marry who your parents want you to. I hate to see this place, that I love so much, bringing you down. Live your own life, son. Be happy."

*Why couldn't Patrick McKinley be my dad? My mom chose the wrong brother, this is certain.*

"Thank you, uncle. I appreciate your concern, but I don't hate this place. Running this team is something I am very proud of. Venture Capitalism may not be my thing, but I found something I can live with and still be a part of the company. It's not perfect, but I'm happy."

It's not a complete lie. I do love parts of my job, and most importantly, it brought me Olivia.

"Well, I'm glad to hear it." He reaches the door and turns to me with the smile I've been told so many times I have. The one that exudes the McKinley charm. "Don't let the old bastard get you down. See you Thursday night."

He shuts the door behind him, and I'm left with my racing mind. My mind that is filled with angry memories of my father, the pride of my uncle's praises, and the tenderness of the woman in the office next door.

All it takes is to think of her concern and worry for me earlier today, and the drama of my father is overshadowed by the grace and beauty of a woman who has brightened up my cold gray world and made it colorful again. Only she comes with more color than I ever knew existed.

I'm not accustomed to someone fretting over me and making a fuss. My parents wouldn't have noticed if I came home bloodied to a pulp. They didn't concern themselves with me. I wonder what Olivia thinks of the fact that I work for my family's company, considering my relationship with them. I must look weak in her eyes. I know it doesn't make sense to me, so how could it to her? I know she doesn't care about my family heritage or money, and she probably thinks I am pathetic and put up with my father for the money. I hope she knows me better than that.

The last few minutes with my father have helped me see what I need to do and that I need to get my plan in motion. My plan which will mean I don't have to hide Olivia any longer and could lead to my eventual freedom from EVC, and my father. I just have to go about it the right way. If there was anyone I was going to trust, it would be her.

Looking at the wall that houses her just on the other side, I will her to hear me when I say, "Soon, very soon, gorgeous."

## CHAPTER EIGHTEEN

*Ronan*

She sparkles inside and out.

It's her big night. *Our* big night.

It's the annual EVC Gala for Children's Cancer Research. I'm doing my very best to keep my distance and give her the professional space she asked for. I'm mingling, kissing ass to all of those who paid a pretty penny to be here and pretending to adore my mother and father.

All the while, my gaze rarely leaves her. She is wearing another one of her perfect little black dresses. Sexy and demure. Sweet and sassy. I'm not sure how anyone in this room could be looking at anything but her.

I love this sweet, professional side of hers, but I can't help but chuckle under my breath when I think of the side I saw of her just last night, when I got home late from New York.

"Hey, handsome."

*I hear her seductive voice from down the hall. I can tell by the way she says those two simple words, she's feeling sassy. Just the way I like her.*

"Where you at, gorgeous?"

"In bed, waiting for you. Come find me."

*Hell yes, my girl is feeling sassy, and I cannot be happier. In situations like this, her sass tends to work out in my favor and hers.*

*"What are you up..."*

*Words escape me when I reach the doorway of her bedroom. The vision in front of me makes any of my boyhood fantasies pale in comparison.*

*The lights are off, and there are candles lit all around the room. The bedding is pulled back, and in the center of it is everything I could have ever dreamed of and more. I don't know how it would be possible to ever want another woman again. I have no idea what I've done to deserve her, but I'm sure as hell never letting her go.*

*Knowing exactly what I like, she has put herself together perfectly. Sitting back on her elbows with one leg bent and the other crossed over it, she knows she's got me. I'm a goner.*

*Her long, chestnut waves are sitting high in a messy pony tail on top of her head, and she has nothing on but one of my ties and her glasses. Her fucking glasses.*

*They get me. Every. Single. Time. She even moves them down her nose just the slightest bit and looks at me from over the top of them like she knows I love. "Do you like?" she asks as the foot attached to her long, sexy, crossed leg bounces up and down, her body shimmering in the dancing flames of the candle.*

*She's pleased with herself.*

*As she should be.*

*"Oh, baby. I love!"*

*Her smile widens, and she flips the navy striped tie resting between her breasts, back and forth and says, "Take it off. All of it."*

*I see...she's taking control. Well, honey you don't have to ask me twice.*

*I may want to rip the suit from my body, but I make a point to take my time. I leisurely remove my jacket, cufflinks, and belt. Next my shoes and socks and then I move on to the parts I can tell she's getting wet for. Her legs may be crossed, but I can still see the glistening coming from that beautiful pussy of mine and it is. All. Mine.*

*Her foot never stops bouncing, but as the clothes come off, she starts biting her bottom lip. This is one of her tells for sure. When that lip is between those teeth, it means she wants whatever it is she's looking at. I will never skip a day at the gym if this is the effect my hard work has on her. Watching her slowly come undone as she tries to hide her squirming to ease the want that is radiating off her body is like a God damn drug and I need her. Now.*

"Did you enjoy the show?"
"Very much so, thank you."
"What next?"

*She uncrosses her legs and spreads her bent legs apart inviting me in.*

*My hard as hell erection bounces on its own accord when I see her drop the tie, letting it fall in front of her beautiful pussy. I don't ever want her to take away that view, but if she's going to do it...naked with her legs spread and my tie as the road block is fine by me.*

*When I finally make it to the bed and touch her, all is right in the world. This is where I am meant to be. We are meant to be, right here. Right now.*

*I crawl over her and take her in a kiss, and when I do, my cock presses against her, rubbing the tie back and forth across her clit. She whimpers into my mouth, and the soft and slow approach we have going is out the window.*

*"Gorgeous, I missed you so much,"* I say as my hand lifts the tie and rests it on her stomach, and I gently start to massage my gift. *"Is this all mine?"*

*"Yes,"* she barely gets out on another whimper. *"I missed you so much, Ronan."*

*She moans at my touch, and I can't wait any longer to taste her. I lick my way down her silky-smooth olive skin and pay my respects to her perfectly taut nipples, making my way down her body and to the promised land. The moment my tongue tastes her, I can't help but growl in lust and possessiveness. I devour her and feel the throb of her orgasm rising as she finds her voice, and my name is a prayer on her lips.*

*While she's still riding high, I cover her body with mine again and slide into what feels like home. She is warm and tight and still contracting from her climax only seconds ago. Her screams become incoherent, and the lust and need we have for each other becomes frenzied. Our speed picks up, and we move in sync together. Her nails rip down my back, and her legs are wrapped tightly around my waist as I take her over and over again.*

*I can feel her tightening, and her breaths are more like gasps for air as she moves closer to the edge again.*

*"Fuck! Gorgeous, you're gonna make me come! Come with me, baby! Fuck! Yes! Just! Like! That!"*

*We both still but our breathing is labored, and I can still feel her throbbing around me. We're both reeling from what just took place. Neither of us speaks. Still inside her, I push her glasses back up her nose and kiss her gently. Her tongue breaks the seam of my lips and finds its way in, and she kisses me deeply. I know what she's trying to tell me with this kiss. I feel the same, and if I didn't think it would scare her away, I would have no problem saying those three words to her. I'm not sure she's ready yet. Maybe once she's heard my plan.*

"I missed you more than I thought I would," she says once I finally roll off her and pull her onto my chest.

"What? You didn't think you would miss me?"

"I knew I would, but I didn't know it would be so hard. I've never really missed anyone before."

*It breaks my heart to hear her say that, but if I take a look in the mirror...neither have I.*

"It's a physical pain for me to be away from you, Olivia. I think you need to start traveling with me. You are my personal assistant after all."

"I don't want to admit you're right, but I may have to reconsider."

"It would produce an entirely new problem, though..." She looks at me with a cocked brow as she lifts her head from my chest. "It would be horrible to sit next to you on a plane or in a boardroom and not be able to touch you. I think our disguise would be foiled. Good thing, I almost have things in place and sooner, rather than later, I may have a solution to our problem."

"Tell me!"

"Nope. Not until it's a done deal and something I think you would be interested in. If you aren't on board with my solution, then it's back to the drawing board, or you just suck it up and we come out, as they say."

"Well, I can't wait to hear what your idea is. I'll be right back."

She knows I am watching her, and as she walks out of the room in the direction of the bathroom, she swings her hips seductively and throws my tie over her shoulder. And just like that, I am ready for round two.

Minutes later, she's back with a warm washcloth and takes her time cleaning me up. Once she settles back *in bed next to me she rolls over onto her side, and I assume my position behind her and wrap her in my arms.*

*"So, talking to you about my mom has had me thinking and...I think I want to try to find her." She lets out a heavy breath, and I can tell it is not an easy decision for her to come to.*

*"Baby, I'll do whatever I can to help you find her. I have a crack team who can find her, and if they can't they'll know who to reach out to, to get the job done.."*

*"I don't expect you to do that for me."*

*"I won't have it any other way. You leave it to me, baby." I kiss the back of her head and feel her body relax and melt into mine.*

*All too soon she stiffens again.*

*"What is it? You can tell me anything," I whisper in her ear.*

*"It's not that big of a deal really. It's just that…um…my birth name is Amber Olivia McCarthy."*

*Amber?*

*"Okay, did your mom remarry or something?" I ask innocently enough.*

*"No."*

*"Okay. No explanation needed. Thanks for letting me know. It will help when the team starts their search for her tomorrow."*

*"My mom had my name changed after my dad passed. Due to the circumstances of his death, she felt it might be safer, and I always liked Olivia better. That's all."*

*That's all? Is she serious? There is clearly more about her father's death that she hasn't told me.*

*I give her a squeeze and kiss her shoulder. "I'm so sorry, baby. Thank you for telling me."*

*When she realizes I am not going to grill her and*

*push her for more information, I feel her body go lax and she settles in for the night.*

*I'm proud of her for coming to this decision. I know it may not be easy and will bring up the ghosts from her past that she has tried so hard to escape, but I'm glad it's something I can help her with. All I want to do is fix all of her broken pieces. Not because she is broken to me. To me, she is perfect, but she has had so much loss and trauma in her life, and I'll do whatever I can to make it all better.*

*She has erased all the gray from my world and has brought all the colors of the God-damned rainbow to my life. It's my turn to return the favor in any way possible.*

"Ronan, are you going to introduce me to the hot little number that's got all of your attention tonight?"

London's voice grates on my nerves when the first syllable leaves her mouth. The shrill sound brings me back to the here and now, and it looks like my feet are moving on their own accord because I've made my way around the room and like always, I'm drawn to Olivia without even realizing it, because I'm now only a few feet away from her.

"Hello, London. Nice to see you."

I lean in and kiss her on the cheek, but she's right; only one person here tonight has all of my attention. I force myself to be polite to London, even though I have come to loathe her. But I learned long ago not to poke the bear.

"Is this the new assistant I've heard so much about?"

London, being London, doesn't just say this to me. No, she's placed herself right in front of Olivia and isn't looking at me, but right at the woman who looks twice as good as she does with half the effort. She's trying to make her uncomfortable, but my girl isn't going to let the likes of London St. James get the best of her.

"Ms. St. James, we've spoken on the phone, but it's so very nice to meet you in person."

Olivia shakes her hand and smiles her megawatt smile, and I can tell London hates her more and more with each passing second.

*Careful, baby. This one bites.*

"Likewise," London says, dismissing her and turning around to face me. "Ooh, listen to that, Ro. It's our song. Dance with me!" She practically squeals, all for effect and to put Olivia in her place.

"Sorry, London. No dancing for me tonight."

*And since when do we have a song?*

Just as she begins her protest, she's cut off at the pass when my uncle rescues me. "Excuse me, ladies. I need to steal my nephew for a moment"

And just like that I'm saved.

Patrick pats my shoulder and says, "I know how you feel about that blonde she-devil, and I thought I'd send you a flotation device. Besides, I may or may not have paid a reporter from *The Times* to follow in my footsteps a moment later to distract her from your girl. We all know how London loves to talk about herself."

*Whoa...what did he just say?*

"I'm sorry, Patrick, my girl?"

"Don't be cute with me, boy. I'm not your father. I can see that what you have with her is the real deal."

*Shit!*

"What gave it away?"

"Son, I know you. You have been surrounded by women dressed to the nines, throwing themselves at you, and your eyes haven't left your assistant all night. At least

I don't think it's Evelyn you've been staring at. I feel like I would have noticed that years ago."

"She's gonna kill me. She really doesn't want anyone to know, and all I want to do is shout it from the mountain top."

"Sounds like you've finally find her, huh?"

"I know I have."

"She wants to keep it private so she doesn't look like she screwed the boss to get her job, right?"

"Exactly."

"You've got to respect that. Especially, if that's not the case."

"It's not. She didn't want anything to do with me and had a boyfriend when I hired her. There was nothing I could do about it, Patrick. It's a first for me. I have never even considered dating or sleeping with one of my employees before. I know it's a bad situation, but I think I've got a solution."

"Well, as long as you're happy, and it doesn't hurt EVC or give your father another reason to blow his top, I say congrats to you and Olivia."

Who knew it would feel so good to talk about my relationship with Olivia out loud. I know I hate keeping it a secret, but I had no idea how much I needed to talk to someone about it.

"Thanks, that means a lot to me."

"Of course, I just want you to be happy. Like I said the other day, I know you don't love working at EVC, even though we gave you your own division. I know it's not your first love."

"Does father know?"

"Your father doesn't care if you are miserable or not, and for that...I am truly sorry. You deserved better growing up, and I wish I was there more for you, kiddo."

"You were there plenty, and I appreciate it more than you know."

"Okay, okay...let's stop with all this sissy stuff and get you back over to your girl. London is nice and distracted. The coast is clear." He turns on his heel and walks away, leaving me to saunter back to Evelyn and Olivia and unfortunately my two best friends.

My uncle isn't the only person I've talked to about Olivia. Richie and Ben, my two closest friends could tell something had me spinning the other night at practice. I told them about Olivia, and they both told me I was crazy. Richie, the CEO of his own accounting firm, went off on me and warned me I was opening myself up to trouble and work place harassment. Ben, wasn't quite as vocal but also expressed his concern. Ben is a police officer and his work being what it is, he is a bigger risk taker than Richie and I, but I could still see he was worried. In the end, these two have been through it all with me, and they believed me when I said I thought I had found the one and what my plan was.

Olivia and Evelyn are in the middle of a conversation with my two idiot friends, and it's no surprise to see she is winning them over with ease. I don't interrupt because I want them to get to know her, but a part of me is worried they may be sharing stories that may not be in my favor. Ben looks up and sees me standing self-assured, with my hands in my pockets, and he gives me a barely-there nod that says he gets it. He knows already what I know: she's worth the risk.

Standing on the sidelines watching the partygoers in all their inauthenticity as they pretentiously kiss each other's asses, I realize how tired I've grown of this world, of these people. Some of them don't even try to hide it when they roll their eyes and start whispering the minute the person they were just talking to walks away. Then there's the sweet brunette headed my way. She is so much better than the rest of us.

She stands next to me, shoulder to shoulder and watches the crowd along with me.

"I see you met Ben and Richie. I hope they didn't try to embarrass me too much?"

"I did meet them, and they did assure me they had many stories they could share with me at lunch next week. They said they wanted to be sure I knew who I was dealing with. We've got a lunch date for next Wednesday."

*Those bastards.*

"Is that so?"

"It is. Ben also seemed very proud to have been the one to give you that black eye at practice last week, but Richie assured me you got him good after."

"That I did."

"You told them."

"I did."

I wait for her to get upset, but she doesn't. We've stopped chatting and watch the crowd. When a slow song comes on, she clears her throat. Trying to be nonchalant, she says out of the corner of her mouth, "Why aren't you dancing? You need to dance, even if it's with London. You look like a bad host if you don't participate."

"If there is a dance to be had, it will be with you. It's you I want in my arms. No. One. Else."

"Oh, my goodness, you are so stubborn. If you're not going to dance, then it's speech time." She nods to Evelyn who walks over to my father and uncle and begins to guide them to the stage.

"Fine by me. Let's get this over with."

"Right this way, *sir*."

*Her and her fucking sass.*
"Careful, gorgeous."

I hear her giggle next to me, and all is right in my world. Dance or no dance, hearing her happy is all I need.

I join my father and uncle on stage, and not wanting the limelight, I let my dad take the reins. He drones on like he gives a shit about the sick kids we're here to raise money for when we all know he's only doing it for the PR and the tax write off.

Once the dog and pony show is over, I'm taking my last step off the stage when the band starts playing. The moment the first few notes of the Van Morrison classic about his brown-eyed girl rings through my ears, I can take it no longer. I stalk toward *my* brown-eyed girl, and I can see the fear in her eyes when she's sees me storming her way.

I hand her phone and tablet to Evelyn and grab her hand, pulling her onto the dance floor. I start swinging her around before she can get more than my name out. I twirl her out in front of me and pull her back in close.

"I'm tired of hiding. It's killing me. Being in the same room with you and not touching you is unbearable."

Not letting her reply, I twirl her away from me and then back in tight.

I'm speaking so only the two of us can hear our conversation, but the intimate way our bodies are pressed together make it clear this isn't a friendly dance. Along the edge of the dance floor, tongues are wagging and the flash of pictures being taken are blinding. I spin her back out and use some of my best moves, and she squeals with joy when she spins around me. I figure if they're all going to watch and document the moment, I might as well put on a good show.

Van Morrison ends, and a slow song comes on. I pull her in nice and close. "You ready to hear my plan?"

"I think now is a pretty good time since I can't show my face at work again."

I've never been so nervous. What if she hates my idea? What if is she's pissed that we didn't come out with our relationship on her terms. I've essentially just outed us, and all her worst fears are coming to fruition.

"I've started a new business, and I want you to run it."

"Excuse me?"

"You heard me. You have a degree in Business Management, and I have every bit of faith in you. And I think you'll like it."

"Start talking, handsome."

"I've started a company called Luna Enterprises."

She smiles because she gets the meaning of the name. This is just another way of sharing my moon with her.

I smile back and give her a conspiratory wink. "It's going to be a business that helps up-and-coming artists. Not just at the gallery in Laguna, but in cities all over the country and abroad. I'm an investor in several galleries on both coasts and in Europe. We will plan events that showcase artists from all parts of the world. I have a vision, and I hope you'll be a part of it. We'll help get new artists out into the art world while continuing to host events to raise money for organizations that mean something to the both of us."

We're moving back and forth to the tempo of the music, but we aren't moving around the dance floor. We're grounded in deep conversation and deciding our future right here in front of everyone at the gala. Not how I had planned it but nothing I can do about it now.

"Ronan, I don't know anything about art."

"But I do...and so does Ava. Besides, you're a quick study and you'll pick it up. What you do know is event planning, and this will essentially be an event planning business for artist events. Not just up-and-comers but established, well-known artists. We'll become the go-to event planners of the art world and both get to work in a business we love."

"Do you have any clients yet?"

"Nope, not a one."

"It doesn't sound like a full-time job, at least not yet. What do I do until then?"

"There's a lot to do to get started, and we need to get our name out there. I have big plans for Luna and my hope is to get it going and eventually leave EVC. I have investments all around the world that are my own and not connected to my father's company. I have my own money, plenty of it. I don't need to work there. It has just always been expected of me. Besides, being with you is worth every penny I have. I would be happy to live as a pauper as long as it's with you, gorgeous."

Her eyes glisten and one lonely tear falls. I wipe it away with my thumb.

"Good tears?"

"Great tears."

Not giving a good God damn about who sees us, including my father, I crash my lips to hers and let everyone in the room know who I'm leaving with tonight.

I may have had to lay my plan out sooner than expected, but I'll figure it out. I'll pay her out of my own pocket for now, even though she doesn't need a paycheck. My reason for living is now to take care of her, whether she knows it or not. My talk with Evelyn earlier today went well, and she is already on board with coming back as my assistant. Now, it's time to groom Allison and Leslie for promotions, and eventually, promote Gloria to VP and someday soon, I'll disconnect myself from EVC for good.

---

## *Olivia*

Silence fills the car as Baxter drives us back to Ronan's. The night was a success with a lot of money being raised for the kids. I couldn't be more pleased, if only the evening wasn't over-shadowed by the uncertainty bubbling within me.

In the moment, out on the dance floor with the world watching, Ronan's plan sounded perfect. I couldn't believe this man had done this for me, for us. But now, here alone in the back seat of the car with his hand in mine, I'm starting to panic.

Since when do I let a man plan my life for me? Should I be pissed that he went and started a company for me to run, without having a single conversation about it with me first? Is this all a part of his plan to make me a *kept* woman? What about that scene on the dance floor? Did he ask me if I wanted to be thrown into the limelight?

When we stepped off the dance floor, and I noticed all the flashes from the photos that were being taken, I was instantly filled with dread that my life was never going to be the same again and the fear that my past may come back to haunt me.

To haunt him.

He should have asked me first. That's really all there is to it. We should have had a private conversation and not one in front of hundreds of people with cameras pointed at us.

I slide my hand from his, breaking our connection. Staring out the window, I can feel him watching me. I know my mood is swinging from one extreme to the other, but once I had a half a second to think about things, the reality of the situation and how it was handled came to light in my head, and I'm not liking what I see.

"Baby, what is it?" he asks quietly, but I don't care to discuss our relationship in front of Baxter. Besides, I think we may be about to have our first fight. We don't need witnesses.

"Not now, Ronan."

Being the perfect man that he always is, he doesn't push. He leaves me alone, and a few minutes later, we're home. Well, we're at his home.

Baxter gets the door for me, and while the two men discuss their plans for the next day, I let myself in. The moment I'm inside the house, I take my shoes off and carry them and my exhausted self upstairs. I grab one of his T-shirts from his walk-in closet—which is bigger than my entire apartment—and as I hear his steps on the stairs, I close myself inside the master bathroom and get ready for bed.

I need to wash my face and clear my head before the conversation that is inevitable occurs. I find my cosmetic bag I had brought over this morning, knowing I was going to stay here tonight, and go through the motions. I remove my contacts, wash my face, brush my teeth and stall as long as humanly possible before I pull up my big girl panties and open the door to face him.

I've rehearsed what I was going to say in my head on a loop since the car ride home. I know exactly what I want to say and the points I need to make. I straighten my back and hold my head up high and swing open the door.

I'm not expecting to be met with the deflated man, sitting on the side of the bed with his head hanging between his shoulders. His jacket and tie are off, and his shirt is untucked, but he doesn't seem to have had it in him to fully change out of his tuxedo. He looks devastated, and before I've said a word, he proves his worth to me just like he always does.

"I never should have outed us the way I did. I am so sorry, Olivia." His head is still aimed at the floor, and his eyes are closed. "I thrust you into my world without even asking you if it was what you wanted or if you were ready for it." He finally lifts his head, and his apologetic eyes meet mine. "I know you want me when it's our little secret, but just because you want me doesn't mean you want everything that comes along with me. I didn't give you a choice tonight, and for that I am truly sorry."

I know I have every right to be pissed right now, but he's just apologized for everything I was going to argue about that part of the evening.

However, there is more to be said.

I take a seat next to him on the bed, but I don't touch him.

"You're right. It should have been handled differently. Thank you for acknowledging that. I have lived my life, looking over my shoulder and just trying my best not to be afraid of my own shadow. Having my picture taken like that wasn't something I was ready for. I would have liked to have been prepared for that."

"I know and I am so very sorry. I hate the way I handled things, and I hope you'll forgive me?"

"I do, but there's more that needs to be discussed."

"What is it? I've already reached out to my team

to try to spin the media and to snag as many of the pictures and videos that we can but, baby, in this day and age there isn't really much I can do to stop the images from getting out there. I wish I could give you more assurance, but I would be lying to you."

"It's the business. You started a new business endeavor that not just involves me, but it means a new job, in a line of work I don't know anything about. It means leaving a place I'm just getting comfortable with and people I'm starting to bond with."

"Olivia..."

"Please let me finish."

"Of course," he says quietly, giving me the floor.

"Ronan, I just leased an apartment based off what EVC was paying me. I hate to even bring this up, but you know that I cannot have you paying for things, and this is a startup business. How do I know I will be able to afford a change like this?"

One corner of his mouth lifts subtly, and I know he thinks I'm silly to worry about money when this isn't something he has to worry about, but it's important to me that I earn my own living. I do my best to disregard his beautiful face and carry on.

"What if we start this, and I don't enjoy it and want out? I don't know that this will be the case but what if it is? I don't want to feel indebted to you and stay on because I feel I owe you. I also don't want to feel kept. I need to know that I am earning what I have on my own. I know you mean well, but I don't need you to take care of me. To go start a new company so we can hold hands when we're out in public. I could have found myself my own job."

"I thought you were happy about Luna. You seemed to be happy when I told you about it. What happened between then and now?"

He has every right to be confused. I was over the moon when he told me his plans, but then the flashing lights of people's cameras in my face startled me back to reality.

"I was happy, but as the night went on, I had time to think about the reality of the situation. You've planned out my entire life without asking for my input. Even if I hadn't been alone most of my life and have the independence issues I do, it stills seems like it would be common courtesy to have involved me. It is *my* life, Ronan."

He pushes up from the bed and starts pacing the plush carpet at our feet. His hands are on his hips, and it seems he's trying to work through everything I've said, but he's coming up short. He rubs his hands over his face and tries to collect himself before facing me and taking his turn to speak.

"I don't get it, Olivia. I've told you all along I was working on a plan. A plan that would let us be together and work together. You knew this was happening. Maybe not the details but I never hid the fact that I was working on something like this. So, where is all of this coming from?"

He's right and he's pissed. His voice rises and now he's yelling.

"And you know something...this wasn't just about *your* life. It's about *our* life...the potential of the two of us having a life together! For some reason, I thought that was what we both wanted! Was I wrong?"

He's right, again. I have only been thinking of myself and not the fact that this is also his path to freedom from his father. The plan means he can leave EVC behind and live his own life and, apparently, he wants to spend it with me.

I meet him in the center of the room and wrap my arms around his middle. I take in his scent and feel his heart pounding beneath my ear. He's upset and rightly so. His arms don't wrap around me until I say, "You're not wrong. I do like the potential of the two of us having a life together. I got scared and all my insecurities came rushing back to the surface." His arms finally come around me, and he squeezes me tightly, kissing the top of my head. "I still think we could have worked this out together, but I get it."

"Baby, there is still so much to do and nothing is set in stone. I want to hear all of your ideas and start from scratch with you. I think we'll make a pretty great team."

"I agree but where will we be based out of?" I ask into his chest. "Who is going to hire and train my replacement at EVC? We need a logo, a website, a—"

Taking a step back and forcing me to look up at him, he does his best to reassure me. "Hey, slow down. We have all the time in the world and no need to worry about a logo and website tonight. We'll start it here at my home office, but really this is a business that can be run anywhere. I'm hoping to work out of Eclipse as often as possible."

"Ooh, that sounds nice."

He smiles agreeing with me. "And you don't need to worry about your replacement. The minute we walked off the dance floor, I got a text from Evelyn. She said retirement was boring her and she would be more than happy to come back. I think she knows you well enough to know you wouldn't want to go back to EVC after your inconsiderate boyfriend outed you in front of the world."

And there it is.

My world is flipping upside down, yet everything

appears to be falling into place.

Even so, I think I better buckle up because this could be a bumpy ride.

## CHAPTER NINETEEN

*Four weeks later*

*Olivia*

The cool San Francisco breeze ruffles the papers on my desk, and I move my moon shaped paperweight on top of the pages to keep them in place. In place on *my* desk in Ronan's office. Ronan's beautiful office that he has handed over to me. This is where I run our new little business, Luna Enterprises.

He tried to give me his desk, but I refused so he had another one sent in for me and put it on the other side of the room. He offered to remodel and add shelves on what is now my side of the room, but I refused. It's perfect the way it is. Especially, when we're sharing the space.

Ronan is still working full time at EVC, and since our secret little business is still a secret, except from Ava and Evelyn, I spend a lot of time here alone, but the owner of Luna does still work from home from time to time, and he does take more lunch breaks than he used to. Although very distracting...I love it when he's here.

The last few weeks we have gotten all the basics done. Website, logo, stationary and supplies order, bank accounts opened, spreadsheets created, and the endless tasks that are involved when starting a brand-new enterprise. We've even found time to have dinner with Ben and Richie and their wives. I've also gone to lunch with Leslie and Allison, and they couldn't have been sweeter about understanding my circumstances.

I've loved every second of our new venture, and the fact that we're doing it together is exhilarating. I really was worried about not enjoying the work and even though we are just in the beginning stages, I think Ronan was right, and I'm going to love this path that we're on. The path he may have set in place, but that we are both navigating together. Side by side, as partners.

I hear the kitchen door, which leads to the garage, close, and when I hear his baritone voice yell, "Honey, I'm home," I get all tingly inside. I still have my apartment, but I'm never there. This multi-million-dollar house has become my home. If you had asked me three or four months ago if this would be my life, I would have laughed in your face. But here I am and here he is.

Here we are.

"Hey, babe. You're home early." It's a Tuesday, and I know he had a day full of meetings so it's odd that he's home already.

When he reaches my desk, he sets some paperwork down and gives me one of his sweet forehead kisses and says, "It's good to see you, gorgeous. I missed you."

"Is that the only reason you're home so early? You missed me?" I can smell the cigarette smoke on him. Something is stressing him out if he's had a smoke.

He smiles but it doesn't reach his eyes. He cups my cheek in his big hand, and he looks like he's trying to form words but he doesn't know how.

I lightly hold on to his wrist and lean my face into his hand. "What is it? Is everything okay?"

Clearing his throat, he finally speaks. "Baby, we found your mom."

There is a sudden thudding in my ears and a twist of anxiety in my gut, and my mouth goes dry. This was not what I was expecting to hear, and by the look on his face, I may not like the rest of what he has to say.

"What's wrong? Does she not want to see me?" I gasp at my next thought. "Is she alive?"

"Sweetheart, she's alive but she's very sick. She's been in hospice care for quite some time, and there may not be much time left. If you want to see her, we need to go soon. Very soon."

I can feel the tears welling in my eyes, and I inhale through my nose to try to keep myself in check. I stand from my chair, and as I walk around the office, I can feel myself shaking from the inside out. I stop in the middle of the room, and the first tear falls. He wraps his arms around me just in time. Without him there to catch me, I most certainly would have fallen.

I brace my hands on his chest, and I take in his scent. Even with the smell of cigarettes, his smell still grounds me. Calms me.

"Where is she?"

"She's in a hospice facility in Southern Oregon."

"What's wrong with her? Is there anything they can do for her? Does she not have insurance?"

"It's cancer, baby."

"What kind?"

Sheepishly, he says, "Lung cancer and money doesn't seem to be a problem. There is a man by the name of Richard Brown paying all of her medical bills."

I still and my body turns to ice.

*It can't be.*

*After all of these years, she's still with him?*

"Dickey," I whisper.

"Who?"

Not ready to go there, I brush past the news that my mother is still under the thumb of the wretched man who put my father in the ground and later abused her day in and day out.

"When can we go?"

"Olivia, who's Dickey?"

"He played a role in my father's death, but I really don't think I can go into more than that right now. Maybe later?" At the mention of his name, I find myself reaching up to touch the small scar above my eyebrow. Courtesy of Dickey Brown.

"Sure, baby. I figured we could fly out in the morning? I've already let the office know I won't be back until Monday, and I've got the plane scheduled to leave bright and early, if that's what you want."

"Yes, thank you."

Inside, I'm screaming to leave this instant. To save her from her disease and from the horrible man still holding her hostage. The man who broke her and took both of my parents away from me. I can't believe she is still with him.

For the next several hours, I busy myself with work, telling Ronan I have a lot to do before we leave. I can tell he's stressed. He is doubting his decision to tell me my mother had been found since she's on her deathbed. He wants to ask more questions about Dickey, and he wants to fix things. Things that he didn't break and he's not responsible for, but I know it's in his nature. It's who he is.

I've been pretending to work, but I'm really just staring blindly at the computer screen. My mind reeling with the knowledge that I'll be seeing my mom in a matter of hours. What if she doesn't want to see me? What if she's so sick she doesn't remember me? What if he's there?

Ronan breaks the barrage of questions racing through my mind when he makes me stop working and eat dinner. It's just the two of us in the house, and the silence between us is deafening. He doesn't want to push too hard, and I don't want to break.

We go through the motions the rest of the night, packing overnight bags, just in case. The tension in the air is thick. I'm exhausted from the emotions of the day and the anxiety of what tomorrow may bring, and all I want to do is sleep.

Escape.

I crawl into bed and Ronan, who always sleeps naked, comes to bed in light blue pajama bottoms. He's trying hard to be respectful and to give me my space. To do the right thing.

## CHAPTER TWENTY

*Ronan*

The smell of disinfectant and bleach cannot be ignored when the automatic doors swoosh open at the hospice center where Susan McCarthy currently resides. The walls are painted with muted, calming colors, and there is soft instrumental music playing. I don't know what I expected, but it feels more like a hospital than I would have thought, and you can feel the weight of death all around you.

Olivia has been a quiet mess all morning, and I don't think she has ceased shaking since I gave her the news that her mother had been found. Before bed last night, I went over the file my team had provided me and reached out to Ben. He contacted the local police department, and when we arrived, I saw the police cruiser already parked in the parking lot. I don't know anything about this Dickey character, but whatever Olivia isn't telling me isn't good, that much I know. Better safe than sorry. The file told me that Richard "Dickey" Brown visits in the evenings. He's usually here between six and seven p.m., so we shouldn't have to worry about any run-ins, but still, you just never know.

I check us in at the front desk while Olivia takes a seat in the lobby. The receptionist hands me a clipboard which requires the date and time, my name, who I'm visiting and my signature. I add my name to the list and join Olivia in the typically uncomfortable waiting room chairs. I take her shaking hand in mine, but I don't know what else to do, and I certainly don't know what to say.

I can't tell her it's going to be okay. She's about to see her mother for the first time in nearly twenty years, and she's dying. It's not okay, none of this is, but at least she will get to see her mother before she passes. This is what I keep telling myself as I sit and hope I am not doing irreparable damage to her.

"Mr. McKinley?"

I rise to my feet, my hand still in hers, but she doesn't stand. She's staying rooted to the spot, and she starts to shake even more, if that is possible. I lift a finger to the nurse to let her know we need a second, and she steps away to give us some privacy.

"Gorgeous, you okay?"

"What if...what if she doesn't want to see me? What if she tells me she hates me? What if I don't recognize her? What if she is so sick she can't talk to me, and I'll never know why she never came for me? What if..."

Pulling her to her feet and into my chest, I'm not sure what to say because one or all of those things could happen. "You're right. We don't know what's going to happen, but what I do know is that I'm going to be right by your side through it all."

She pulls away so she can look at me with those beautiful doe eyes of hers. She's searching my face as if she's not sure if I'm real. She really has been on her own since she was a small child. This is all new to her. It's tragic that a person filled with so much good has spent her life without receiving it in return. No more. Not on my watch.

"Baby, we share a moon, so you won't ever be alone again. Whatever you need, I'm here. I'm not going anywhere."

The mention of our moon lifts the corner of her mouth ever so slightly. She lifts up her pinky finger, and without hesitation, I seal my fate to the woman before me. It may just be a pinky swear, but to me...it's binding. I will do everything in my power to take care of her, no matter what it takes.

"Okay, let's go," she whispers on an exhale.

Hand in hand, we follow the nurse as she leads us down the quiet halls filled with souls on the verge of heading on to their next life, wherever that may be. Most are alone, and it is tragic to see those who are both young *and* alone. This building made of strong stone and wood is making me feel weak and wilted. I hope I haven't made a terrible mistake. Maybe this isn't how she should finally see her mother again, but here we are. No turning back now.

"This is her," the nurse says outside of room 127.

The door is already open, and in the middle of the room is a tiny woman with dark brown hair. Her hands are folded together, and if I didn't hear the beeping of the machine attached to her, I would think she had already passed. She looks fragile, and it's clear she's been through a lot in her lifetime.

The nurse approaches Susan's bedside and tries to get her attention. She seems to be looking out the window and hasn't noticed our presence. Gently rubbing her arm, the nurse says, "Susan, you've got some visitors." Still no reaction. "I'm sorry, dear, what was your name?" she asks my shaking beauty.

Clearing her throat, she manages to squeak out her name. "Olivia."

Susan's head slowly turns toward the door and one slim hand lifts toward her.

Olivia lets go of my hand and rushes to her mother's side. "Mom," she says, gently taking her mother's frail hand in hers.

Standing beside her, not leaving her side as promised, I gently stroke her back. I have no idea if this is what she wants. I just want her to know I'm here.

"My sweet girl," the frail woman can barely get out on a whisper.

Not replying, Olivia simply takes her thumb to wipe the tears that have fallen from Susan's eyes.

"Sweet girl, you are beautiful." She lifts her hand and reaches for Olivia's face. Olivia leans forward so she can touch her. "I never thought I would see you again. Is this a dream?"

"It's not a dream. I'm really here. I've missed you."

"Oh, sweet girl, I have missed you every day. You are the first thing I think about when I wake and the last vision I see when I close my eyes at night. Please tell me you are happy and well?"

Turning to me with a small smile and a little blush, she says, "I am, Momma, I am so happy. Mom, this is Ronan."

I stop touching Olivia so that I can reach in front of her and take Susan's hand. It's startling how important it is to me to make a good first impression. I'm meeting Olivia's one and only parent. I need her to know her daughter is taken care of.

"It's a pleasure to meet you, Susan."

"Well, aren't you handsome? Are you taking good care of my girl?"

"I am certainly trying. She's mighty independent,

this one." I motion my head toward Olivia. "You're her mother. Please tell her it's okay to let me spoil her."

A smile lights the woman's face. "Oh, I like him, honey, and he seems to like you too. He's a keeper."

"I'm a lucky man to have your daughter in my life, ma'am. She's brilliant, beautiful, kind, and sassy. It's more than like. She couldn't get rid of me if she tried."

The moment the last sentence leaves my mouth, her expression darkens, and fear coats her entire body. It's almost atmospheric. Dropping her hand, I take Olivia's and she says, "Mom, what is it?"

"Diane, what time is it?" she says louder than she has been since we entered the room, and her question leaves her in a coughing fit. Diane brings her a cup with a straw in it and lifts it to her to try to help with the cough. "It's morning, Susan. It's ten fifteen. Why, darlin'?"

After what feels like forever, but is really only a couple of minutes, her coughing fit subsides, and Susan lies in her bed, her tiny body breathing fiercely, looking exhausted. Once she regains her breath, she turns to Olivia.

"Can I have a moment alone with my daughter please?"

"Of course, Susan. I'll be right outside if you need anything. If she has a hard time breathing, just lift her oxygen mask over her mouth and nose, like this. She doesn't talk much, and it can wear her out."

"Okay." Oliva agrees to Diane's request but it's obvious she sounds unsure if she is up to the task.

"Me too. I'll give you ladies a moment."

With panic in her voice, my gorgeous girl is the next to be overtaken by fear. She squeezes my hand, and when her eyes connect with mine, she is practically begging, and I can hear her plea before she says, "Please stay."

"If that's what you want?"

"It is."

I wrap my arm around her shoulders, pulling her into my side, and kiss her head. "I'm here, baby."

Susan smiles a small smile, and once she's hears the click of the door signifying we are alone, she pats the side of the bed, asking Olivia to sit.

I stand next to her holding her right hand while her mother holds her left.

"Sweet girl, I am so sorry. I am so sorry I never came for you, but I couldn't." She takes a few ragged breaths. "Does he know?"

"Yes, he knows almost everything. There's nothing he can't hear."

I know now isn't the appropriate time to feel fucking high as a kite that my girl has just confirmed I am her person. The one she can trust with all of her ghosts and the past that has haunted her for years. I know it's not appropriate, standing next to her dying mother, but damn I can't help it. It feels good.

Olivia, lifts the oxygen mask around Susan's throat to her mouth, and the room is filled with the sounds of the machines monitoring her heart while we wait to hear what she's going to say next. The pieces of Olivia's past that she needs to complete her puzzle. Mother and daughter never break their stare, and eventually, Susan gives an ever-so-slight nod and signals her to remove the mask.

"Olivia, it isn't safe for you to be here."

"I know, momma."

*Wait. What? I didn't know that. I mean I know Dickey is clearly trouble, but what the hell does she mean my girl isn't safe here?*

"Sweetheart, you are the last living witness to your father's murder. You saw so much that day. You went through more than any adult, let alone child should ever go through. If he finds you..." she trails off, deep in thought, coming back to herself a few seconds later. "If he finds you, he will kill you. You really shouldn't have come here."

I am so many things right now.

I am broken, knowing that at six years old, the woman who is my everything witnessed her father's murder.

I am angry as hell that I brought her into a potentially dangerous situation, and she knew and let me do it anyway.

I am overwrought with protectiveness and want to grab her and run out the doors and take her home to safety.

I am determined to find the wretch that has ruined the lives of these two women and bury him six feet underground.

"I had to see you again."

"And, I'm so glad you came. I just don't want you to get hurt. I also hate for you to see me like this."

"Oh, Momma, you still look beautiful." She lightly smooths her mother's hair. "I'm so sorry I didn't find you sooner.

"I hope you know that I had to let the police take you. I had heard him talking, and it was only a matter of time before he was going to do to you what he did to me. I couldn't let you live a life of addiction, prostitution, and abuse." She stops to cough, and Olivia gives her more oxygen.

"It's okay, I survived. I just missed you."

When the mask is removed, her mother continues

her confession. "I was arrested the day they took you, and before Dickey got there to bail me out, I made sure that I gave the officers your information so that when they registered your name with the state, it would be your new name, and he wouldn't be able to find you. I think you're the only reason he's let me live as long as he has. He's been waiting for you to find me. As much as I've dreamed of seeing you again, I still hoped you would never find me."

Susan's breathing is labored, and their short conversation is taking its toll on her. Her mask is back in place but it doesn't seem to be working as well this time.

"Momma, you don't have to say anymore. I am so sorry you have had to endure all of these years of pain and misery. I understand and thank you for protecting me. I'm living my dreams, and it's all because of you. I went to college and got my degree, like you always told me I would. I'm an event planner and I love it. I have an amazing man in my life, and things are really, really good. I owe it all to you."

I squeeze her hand and let her know that she's doing the right thing. Telling her mother all of the high points of her life and not how hard it was for her to get there. At the end of her life of sacrifice, her mother doesn't need to hear the rest. She needs to see the outcome of all that she gave up and that it was worth it. Olivia was worth it.

Susan fumbles to take her mask off and Olivia reaches up to get it for her.

"Thank you for this. I feel like I can go now. I know you're okay and you have someone you love and who loves you back. You aren't alone and you're happy. That is all I ever wanted for you, sweet girl." She turns her cloudy eyes to me. "You keep her safe and happy."

It's an order, not a question.

"There is nothing more important to me in this world. I promise you that, ma'am." I felt Olivia startle when her mom mentioned us loving each other. I know she was worried it would scare me, but her mom knows what she's talking about. We may not have said it, but I love Susan McCarthy's daughter with everything I am.

She gives an almost invisible nod to her head, and she looks back to her daughter. "You need to go, Olivia. Go and don't come back. Know that I love you and that I never wanted to give you up. You were my world, and I am so proud of the woman you have become."

"But I just found you," Olivia cries.

"I've always been with you and always will be. Remember what I always told you...never make yourself small for anybody. Be strong and be proud."

"I remember, Momma."

Yes, she sure does remember that. I can see where her independence comes from now. I know much of it is of her own strength, but some if it clearly comes from her mother.

"Good. Now go..." She coughs again, and I take the break in conversation to try to pull on Olivia's hand and let her know we really should get the hell out of here. I'm itching to get her to safety. "I love you, Olivia, but you have to go."

"Gorgeous, let's go," I whisper softly into her hair, kissing her head.

Leaning forward, she kisses her mother on the forehead and speaks through her tears. "Thank you for everything, Momma. I love you so much."

"I love you too, my sweet girl."

Her mother looks at me as if begging me to take her away.

"Come on, baby. We need to go."

She doesn't speak as I walk her from the room by her shoulders. She looks back, getting every last second of vision of her mother before we are finally out of the room. I can feel her holding on by a thread, and I am so glad that Baxter came along and is waiting in the car. There is no way I can let go of her now.

On our way out, I leave my business card with the front desk and ask that they call me if anything changes. We reach the car, and I exchange a look with Baxter, and he understands we need quiet. He's come to care about Olivia, and I know now that I need to share Olivia's story with him. He's not just my driver, he's also head of security, and he needs to know our situation has just gone to a new and different kind of threat level.

"Baby, I had gotten us a room here for the night, but if you would rather go home we can call and get the plane ready."

"Home. Can we just go home?"

---

All the way home on the plane, she was silent. She lay with her head in my lap and didn't speak a word. There was more silence in the car that left my mind reeling with how I could take care of her. How I could make it better.

When we were on the plane, it occurred to me that my information was on the clipboard in the front desk. I know Olivia's information was nowhere to be found, but what if Diane mentions Olivia's visit when Dickey is there later today? Shit, I hope he doesn't watch the nightly entertainment shows and hasn't seen the footage of Olivia and me at the gala, or at the beach, or the grocery store. We seem to be photographed everywhere we go. London St. James's ex-boyfriend—who still occasionally escorts her to red carpet events—has finally moved on with his personal assistant. At least that's what the tabloids said when the first gala pictures came out.

There isn't anything I can do about any of that now, but I have alerted my security team, and it's all hands on deck to get eyes on Dickey Brown. We need to find him and know his whereabouts at all times. I know Olivia thinks less is more, but in times like this, I am so grateful to have a lot of the more so that I can spare no expense at keeping her safe. Baxter and I were texting during the flight, trying to keep things quiet for her. I didn't need her to hear how frantic I felt. Baxter's got his team on the case, and I trust him to track down Olivia's ghost and help me bury him once and for all.

We're finally home, and as if on autopilot, she takes the stairs to the master suite and lies on top of the bed fully dressed. Her eyes are wide awake, but she is exhausted, and I know she needs to sleep.

I draw a bath for her, and once the tub is filled with bubbles and perfectly hot water, I guide her into the bathroom and take her clothes off. Before stepping into the tub, she wraps her naked body around me and finally speaks.

"Thank you," is all she says but it's enough.

Once she is settled in the water, I sit on the side of the bath and leisurely wash and condition her hair. I gently wash her and then let her lie back and relax until the water grows tepid. I help her out of the tub, dry her off, and cover her in her favorite lotions. As much as I love touching her, there is nothing sexual about this moment. It is about me taking care of her and helping her find her way through all of the emotions brought to the surface today. When she does find her way through to the other side, I'll be here waiting for her.

It's early but bed and sleep is what she needs right now. I put her in one of my Henley's, which have become her new favorite sleepwear, and tuck her into bed. Before long she is out, and once I know she is sound asleep, I head to my office and call Baxter to fill him in on the rest of the details I didn't dare share by text. I tell him her story, and as much as I know she wouldn't want it to be shared, I have to. It's for her safety. I can hear the anger along with empathy in my head of security's voice as well as a determination when he vows to help keep her safe.

I work in my office for an hour or so but, eventually, head to the kitchen patio for a smoke. I stop at the cupboard in the kitchen where I hide them behind the coffee that I never make—kinda hard to hide from myself when I'm the one who put them there—and lean up against one of the columns and think about today and the what-could-have-beens. I will forever be grateful to Susan for not coming to find Olivia. For changing her name and doing what she could to prevent a life of misery and abuse.

To think Olivia could have had this fate on top of witnessing her father's murder and whatever else came with that wretched day, bouncing around from foster home to foster home. Living on her own, in shelters, with no money and putting herself through school. It's no wonder she found a relationship with Bryce. There was nothing to fear. She still got to hide in her protective shell and take care of herself on her own terms. That way she couldn't get hurt, and the only person who could let her down, was her.

I know her letting me in is a big deal, and I will

never take that for granted. I know how it feels to finally have found your person in life, because she is my person. She is the air that I breathe, the color that I never knew existed, and she is mine.

The yellow flame from my lighter lights up the dark patio, and I take my first puff of nicotine. Feeling the sting of the smoke in my throat relaxes me enough to clear my head and think about what she needs next. Food. She hasn't eaten in well over twenty-four hours...since the news that we had found her mother. She pushed food around her plate last night at dinner, but she didn't really eat. Putting out the butt of my cigarette, I watch as the smoke billows lightly through the air, and I know I need to stop. After seeing what the disease has done to Olivia's mother, it would be dismissive and thoughtless of me to continue smoking. I really need to work on my nasty little way of dealing with stress.

I wash up and go about putting together what has become our new go-to dinner. A simple platter of aged cheese, apples, salami, crackers, and some sweet fig spread to go with it. We usually include wine with our meal, but I'm not sure what she'll want tonight. I'll let her decide. I find a serving tray in the pantry and load it up and take the stairs to my sleeping beauty.

When I get there she's awake. She's sitting up in bed and staring into space, looking lost. When she sees me, she smiles. "Hey, whatcha got there?"

"Well, since you haven't eaten in over twenty-four hours, I thought a snack might be in order."

Setting the tray next to her on the bed, I sit down by her feet. She pulls her legs in and crosses them in front of her and slides the tray between us. I follow her lead and sit cross-legged too.

"Ronan, thank you. For everything."

"Of course, baby. I'd do anything for you."

She looks at me with eyes full of tears that have yet to fall, and my heart hurts for her.

"You will never know what it means to me to have gotten a chance to see her again. To know she didn't abandon me. She saved me. She still loves me. You have given me such a gift, my mom as well. She got to see that I'm doing well and that I made it." She wipes away the tears that she couldn't hold back any longer. "Thank you for giving us both so much today. I can never thank you enough, and I will never be able to repay your kindness."

"I'm just glad we were able to find her." Then it hits me. "I know how you can repay me."

"Really, right now? Let me get some food in my stomach and build up some strength first." She throws me a wink.

"Stop with the sass, for just a second." I'm so glad she seems to be coming back to life, and my Olivia is finding her way back to me.

"Yes, sir." She smiles widely.

There she is.

"Move in with me."

"What?" She chokes on her apple.

"Shit, drinks. I forgot drinks. Let me go get you something. Wine, water...what can I get you."

"Uh...I think wine is in order."

I've surprised her. Hell, I've surprised myself, but I know it's right. I know I want to fall asleep with her in my arms every night and the thought of her living alone with a madman after her is unbearable.

"Okay, wine it is. I'll go get it, and while I'm gone you think about it. Well, there's no real thinking about it. You're going to move out of your apartment and you're moving in with me. This is your home, Olivia. Where you belong. MTB, baby." I hurry out of the room before she starts to argue with me.

She laughs at my reference to us being meant to be and yells, "Very cute, now get me my wine and let me think about your very gracious offer."

All I can think, as I practically skip down the stairs, is that she didn't say no! She's thinking about it, and that is more than I expected. I find myself rushing to get back to her and to hear her answer. I grab her favorite white out of the fridge, two wine glasses, and a corkscrew. I've just got it all balanced in my hands when my phone rings in my pocket. I place the wine on the counter and see it's a number I don't recognize.

"Hello."

"Mr. McKinley?" asks the woman on the other line.

"This is he."

"This is Cassandra at Wildwoods Hospice, and I'm calling to inform you that Susan McCarthy has passed. We know you were just here this morning and had asked to be kept updated, so I thought I would call."

"Yes, thank you very much for calling. What happened?"

"Sir, it was simply her time. She'd been sick for quite some time, and it was a miracle she was able to visit with you today. I think your visit was a blessing to her, sir. It was what she needed before she could go."

"Thank you, Cassandra. I appreciate the call."

I hang up and text Baxter with an update. He'll know what to do next. I know that without Susan to use as bait for Olivia to come visit, he will be working even harder to find her on his own now. We need to get ahead of this.

I grab everything from the counter, only now my

pace has slowed. I have to go tell the love of my life that her mother is dead. Her mother that she just saw for the first time in twenty years this morning has passed. I feel sick to my stomach, and when I enter the bedroom and see her sitting on her heels practically bouncing up and down with excitement, I know I am about to ruin her joy. I am about to take that bounce and that smile away.

The second I cross the threshold to the master suite, she says, "Okay."

Forgetting what I had been so excited about mere moments ago, I am overwhelmed for a fleeting moment with joy and relief.

"Is that a yes? You'll move in?"

"It's a yes, handsome! What the hell, we only live once, right?"

At the mention of life, the somber news I have to share is back in a flash.

"That's great news, baby." I set everything down on the bedside table and lean forward to give her a forehead kiss. I grab the chair from the corner of the room and slide it over to the side of the bed where her bounce is starting to fade. She can tell something's wrong. I take a seat. "Olivia, I got a phone call from the hospice center when I was downstairs."

"And..."

"And I'm sorry, baby, but she's gone. Your mom passed today."

Her joy deflates and confusion colors her face.

"But we were just there this morning. How can she be dead?"

"The woman on the phone said that it was a miracle she was even able to speak to us today and that our visit was a blessing."

"But I just found her, Ronan."

Her first tear falls, and I move the tray to the floor and join her on the bed, before taking her in my arms. "I know, baby. I know."

For the next thirty minutes, she sobs in my arms. She cries for the loss, the lifetime of misery her mother endured, and the time she was robbed of with her.

She cries and cries.

To hold the person you love, in your arms while they sob with grief is binding. I feel connected to this woman in a way I never have with any other person before or ever will. She is exposed and vulnerable, and it is me she turns to. Me she trusts with her pain.

Eventually, her tears dry and her breaths are no longer gasps for air. She pushes off my chest so she can look at me, and to see her beautiful eyes so sunken and hollow is one of the hardest things I have ever had to look at. To see her in this kind of pain and to know there isn't a damn thing I can do about it is gut-wrenching.

"I'm sorry you had to deal with all this. I know it was a lot. More than I'm sure you bargained for."

I'm not sure she gets what is happening here, and I want to be sure not another second passes that she isn't crystal clear.

"I love you, Olivia Adams, and I would give anything to take away your pain. Please don't ever feel sorry for leaning on me in your time of need. Your well-being is my number one concern. You are my life, gorgeous, and you will always come first. Whatever you need from me is yours to take."

Her face is no longer dry of tears as new ones start to fall. Her soft hand rubs my check and then slowly outlines my jaw. "I love you too, Ronan."

I need nothing more from this life. To be loved by this woman is more than I could ever ask for. It doesn't get any better than this.

## CHAPTER TWENTY-ONE

*Olivia*

Stretching myself awake, I reach over to find Ronan's side of the bed empty. That's right, he didn't come home last night. There was an emergency at EVC, and he had to head to New York for last-minute meetings.

The last forty-eight hours comes back to me in a rush. Flying to Oregon to visit my mother. To see her and to hear her say she did love me and that she had never truly abandoned me was what I needed to hear. But to lose her the very same day I had just gotten her back was almost too much to take. It was a roller coaster ride, and Ronan was by my side the entire time. Just like he said he would be.

It may not have been the most romantic of moments to confess our love to one another, but it was our moment. He held me all night, and when I asked him to please make love to me, he did just that. We made love slowly, reverently, and it was beautiful. What I have with him is beautiful, or MTB as he now likes to call it.

I slept in his arms all night, and then he stayed home in bed with me all day yesterday. He let me explore every mood I was feeling. From laughing at a rom-com on the TV to bursting into tears at any given minute. By the time he left me last night, I was already feeling almost back to normal. It's hard to imagine as I lie in this big bed that I live here now, or will very soon anyway.

He hated to leave me last night, but I made him. It was his mother's birthday celebration, and he needed to go. I know they aren't close, but it's still his mother, and I don't want him to have any regrets. I was in no shape to go, and I don't think I will ever be ready for dinner at the McKinley's.

Late in the evening, I got a text from him saying that he wouldn't be home and had to take a red-eye to New York. The text told me he loved me, and he signed it MTB yours, Ronan. It's so strange to be grieving the loss of my mother yet be floating on cloud nine in love with the man that was never in my dreams. To think I had such contempt for him during our first meeting on the boat. He really is so much more than I could have ever imagined.

My phone pings, alerting me to a message, and when I go to grab my phone off the bed-side table, it barely budges because Ronan, always thoughtful and looking out for me, plugged my phone in for me before he left. I unplug it and put on my glasses to find a message from Evelyn asking me to meet her for coffee. She said she understands I don't want to come into my old office, and she would meet me at the coffee shop in the building next to EVC.

Hmm...I wonder what this is all about? What could Evelyn need to talk about that would require me to see her in person? We can do almost everything via phone or online so it must be important. I've got about an hour and a half to shower, get dressed, and get myself there in Monday morning traffic, so I drag my well-rested yet emotionally exhausted butt out of bed.

An hour and twenty minutes later, I'm waiting at the crosswalk for the light to change and admiring the beautiful day. There is a chill in the air, but the skies are blue and the sun is out. The bay area clouds have receded, and I'm hopeful this means things are looking up.

The light finally changes, and I'm only a couple of steps from the curb when a motorcycle comes flying by and nearly runs me over. Screaming, I leap onto the curb, and when I look over my shoulder to get a look at the asshole who nearly took me out, he's looking back over his shoulder at me too. Almost like he knew me or meant to scare me on purpose.

"Ma'am, are you okay?" An older gentleman asks, looking me over from head to toe to make sure I'm still in one piece.

"I'm fine, thank you." I lie. I may not be injured but something about that didn't feel right. When I saw the guy on the motorcycle looking back at me the way he did, a chill went down my spine that shook me to my bones.

Finding my balance in my heels and smoothing the front of my skirt, I pull myself together and the kind man offering me assistance moves on his way. Walking through the front doors of the coffee shop right next door to EVC adds another set of nerves to my already shaking body. The tall black building almost looks ominous on this beautiful day. There isn't anything that Evelyn can tell me that will compare to what I've already been through these last couple of days, so at least there's that.

Evelyn is waiting for me at a corner table near the window, and although she looks lovely as ever with her purple scarf peeking out of her jacket, she looks tired or almost heartbroken. She stands when I enter the room and offers her hand.

*A handshake and not a hug? That's odd.*

"Good morning, my dear. I'm very sorry to have called you at the last minute like this."

"Don't give it another thought. It's great to see you." I smile, but inside I feel as though my world may be about to slip away.

"I don't really know how to say this."

"What is it, Evelyn? Is Ronan okay? Has something happened to him?"

"No, nothing like that."

She opens the folder sitting in front of her and takes out a piece of paper and slides it over to me and places a pen next to it.

At the top of the page I see the words NOTICE OF TERMINATION and my heart drops to my stomach.

"I don't understand. I resigned, I don't work for EVC any longer."

"I know that dear. This is a termination notice for Luna Enterprises. As you will see in the letter, Mr. McKinley would like you to leave your laptop and keys and have your things out of his home today if possible."

With tears filling my eyes for the thousandth time in the last forty-eight hours, I look up at her in despair. "I don't understand, Evelyn? What is going on? What did I do?"

"I am so very sorry, dear. I don't have any details, but I do know it's important to Mr. McKinley that you are taken care of. As you'll see in the letter, there is a year's salary already direct-deposited into your checking account, and you will have health insurance for a full year or until you find employment elsewhere." There are tears in her eyes, and I can tell it pains her to have to be the one to do this.

Why is he doing this to her? Why make her do his dirty work? One minute he's telling me he loves me, and the next he has one of his employees break up with me. This cannot be happening.

"Olivia, if you can please sign on the line at the bottom of the page, we'll be all settled here," she says, sniffling.

Looking down on the now tear-soaked page, I sign my name and pull my laptop out of my bag. I place it and his house key on the table. "He can just throw my things away. I don't think I can bring myself to go back there. I'm sorry he wasn't man enough to do this himself and that you were stuck being the bad guy, Evelyn. Thank you for everything, I learned a lot from you. Now if you'll excuse me."

I rise on feeble legs which currently carry a body that has been through too much these last few days. Too many highs and way too many lows. It's more than a person should have to manage. Evelyn stands and pulls me into a strong hug.

She releases me, and I don't hesitate for a single moment when I turn on my heels to leave. When the bell above the door chimes as I cross the threshold, it sounds distant. In slow-motion, I follow my path back across the street and manage to make it to the other side of the crosswalk without being sideswiped by a motorcycle.

Luckily, my apartment is close by, and I only have a few minutes to go before I reach the privacy of my little one-bedroom apartment where I can shatter into a million little pieces.

To Be Continued...

Find out what happens next in
**GORGEOUS: BOOK TWO**


WWW.LISASHELBY.COM

# Gorgeous
BOOK TWO

# GORGEOUS: BOOK TWO
(The Gorgeous Duet)

Ronan was the knight in shining armor she had never dreamed of or needed, and Olivia was the color in his cold gray life.

He loved her sass, and much to her surprise, she didn't mind when he took control.

They shared a moon.

They were meant to be.

Until the nightmares of their pasts rock their newfound happiness putting the magic they share to the test.

They'll soon discover if they have what it takes to fight their way back to each other. To set each other free and share their moon, once again.

---

## **PLAYLIST**

Gorgeous (Live – Upstate Sessions) – X Ambassadors
Sit Still, Look Pretty – Daya
Cold, Cold Man – Saint Motel
Classic Man – Jidenna (feat. Roman GianArthur)
No Roots – Alice Merton
Latch - Disclosure (feat. Sam Smith)
Told You So - Miguel
Redbone – Childish Gambino
Stuck With Me – Timeflies
When You Move – Parachute
Until You – Dave Barnes
Nobody Has to Know – Timeflies
If I Didn't Know You – Nick Fradiani
She Burns – Foy Vance
Moanin' and Groanin' – Bill Withers
Brown Eyed Girl – Van Morrison
Nothing Fancy - Dave Barnes
There Will Be Time – Mumford & Sons & Baba Maal

Spotlink: http://spoti.fi/2CfWc5x

All of my love and appreciation...

It doesn't matter how many books I will write or how many times I thank him, my husband will never know what he means to me. He couldn't be more supportive, is my sounding board and the only person that can talk me down off that 'I suck and don't have a clue what I'm doing' edge. He reminds me every day why I got into this to begin with. It wasn't to be rich and famous but to tell the love stories that I just had to tell. He is my inspiration and I would never have written a single word without him. I love you more, baby. #MTB

My son is the coolest kid on earth and I could not be prouder of him. He is one of the people in my life that gives me faith that there is still good out in the world and that our future is still pretty bright if there are hearts like his out in the universe.

Nadia, as always thank you for my beautiful cover, updated website, and most of all your friendship. I couldn't do it without you. I think we both deserve a drink! Happy hour?

Allison, what would I do without you there to talk all things books, movies and TV? Thank you for putting up with me on the daily and for always keeping it real. Love you, lady.

Lia at Finishing Touch Editing and Tandy at Tandy Proofreads thank you both for helping to make my latest book baby as 'gorgeous' as it is. I cannot thank you enough.

Not sure I can there are words that say exactly what my readers mean to me. Every person that has read one of my books had taken a leap of faith and given a new author a chance. This may be my fourth book but I am still a newbie and I can never thank each and every reader thank you enough. Whether you leave reviews or you don't the fact that you read one word that I have written still blows my mind. Thank you, thank you, thank you!

To all the bloggers and PA's who have helped spread the word about my books, you all hold a special place in my heart. As an indie author, I know that every single one of you that takes the time to share sales, new releases and your reviews, is giving of your time that is being pulled in a million different directions. You have so many books and authors you can promote and the fact that any of you have used your precious time to promote my work is an amazing feeling. Thank you.

Deb Carroll, you are a force. Roni, Missy & Korina how lucky am I to know you ladies? Stacy, you are a crazy cool sister and have become an amazing promotor for my books (even if you haven't read them yet). Love you, sis. I started to list all of my friends and family who have shown their support, in so many different ways, and I just couldn't. There are too many of you and yes, I know I am the luckiest girl in the world. Thank you to each and every one of you who have done nothing but support my journey.

My love and appreciation to the entire romance community. I am so proud to consider myself a part of this amazing group of people.

L

## ALSO BY LISA SHELBY

The You & Me Series
(a sweet and sexy series of adult contemporary standalones.)

You & Me

More

Something Just Like This

———

The Gorgeous Duet

Gorgeous: Book One

Gorgeous: Book Two

Visit
**WWW.LISASHELBY.COM**
to shop for these titles

also available at all major online retail outlets

# **NEWSLETTER**

### NEWS · UPDATES & FREEBIES!

Don't forget to sign up for LoveGeek Monthly.

# WWW.LISASHELBY.COM

# ABOUT THE AUTHOR

Lisa Shelby is an ever-so-hopeless romantic and self-professed love geek. Born and raised in the Pacific Northwest and proud to call Oregon home. It's here that she resides with her husband, son, and two fur baby dogs. Reading has been her obsession and writing had been her secret passion. It was that passion that led her on her journey to write a book for her husband. What began as a gift turned into an inspiration of love and the desire to share that love with everyone. With the encouragement of her husband and the support of her family and friends, she began her journey and published her debut novel, "You & Me" in September 2016. With the completion of her Gorgeous Duet in early 2018, she will have five published works under her belt with an endless amount of ideas and outlines always in the works.

Lisa loves to talk all things books and romance and loves to chat with readers. Be sure to follow her everywhere!

**WWW.LISASHELBY.COM**

@LISASHELBYBOOKS

**BOOKBUB**
www.bookbub.com/profile/lisa-shelby

**BOOK + MAIN BITES**
www.bookandmainbites.com/users/17508

Made in the USA
Lexington, KY
31 October 2019